MW01706687

To Ellen Vanstone
with much affection
& warmth,
- love -
[illegible]
March 1993.

THE MALE OF THE SPECIES

THE MALE OF THE SPECIES

a novel
by
MATTHEW HART

CORMORANT BOOKS

Copyright © Matthew Hart, 1993

Published with the assistance of the Canada Council, the Ontario Arts Council, and the Government of Ontario through the Ministry of Culture and Communications.

The author wishes to acknowledge the support of the Ontario Arts Council and the Canada Council.

Front cover from an oil on canvas by Alex Livingston, untitled, 1988, 151.5 x 205.5 x 3 cm, from the collection of The Canada Council Art Bank, courtesy of the artist.

Cover design by Artcetera Graphics, Dunvegan, Ontario.

Typeset by Moveable Type Inc., Toronto, Ontario.

Published by Cormorant Books Inc.,
RR #1, Dunvegan, Ontario, Canada K0C 1J0.

Printed and bound in Canada.

Canadian Cataloguing in Publication Data

Hart, Matthew, 1945–
The male of the species

ISBN 0-920953-90-5

1. Title.

PS8565.A666M35 1993 C813'.54 C93-090037-5
PR9199.3.H37M35 1993

To Kathleen

"Bless me, Father," mumbled Dave, "it is many years since my last confession. What I need to know is, would it be a sin to inseminate a Protestant?"

"Excuse, my English is not good," said the priest. "What have you said?"

"The seed of the male yearns to be spread, Father," Dave explained. Through the grate he could see the priest, a familiar shape of slick hair and heavy glasses. Around the priest's neck went the thin purple band of a stole. The vestment ended in his lap, a fringe of gold thread against a black cassock. His stubby fingers toyed with the fringe. Dave could see him slide his eyes towards the grate.

"A Protestant is not legally baptized, Father," he said, pulling back into the shadows so the priest could not see his face. "They are in a state of sin anyway, so I don't think it would bother God. I mean, casting seed into one. If that Protestant didn't care about how fornication is supposed to be a sacrament, then God would probably not mind either."

"You are this same boy who was here last week?"

"Not me. I'm visiting from Calcutta."

"How old have you, my son?"

"I'm a fully baptized Catholic, Father."

"What is your sin, my son?" sighed the priest. "You must be exact."

"I'm sort of thinking about copulation."

"*Ah, non*," moaned the priest.

"I'm trying not to say 'fuck', Father."

The priest grunted. Dave could smell his hair lotion. "This is a blasphemy, my son."

"It's a legal English word, Father."

"This would be a horrible sin," said the priest, raising his hands and letting them fall in his lap.

"They don't believe in the Pope," added Dave, still hoping for ecclesiastical sanction. "The act of inseminating the female, it's not that bad for a Protestant."

"How old have you?" asked the priest again, making a new attempt to see him through the grate.

"I have to go, Father."

*

This boy was Dave Swan, hurrying now out of the dim church, out of the choking scent of lavender, the rows of sin-intoxicated widows waiting for their priest; out of all that and into a hot white day and the sensible smell of dust. His younger brother Bill sat on the church steps, a dictionary open in his lap. Bill was too young for sin. He had not reached the age of reason decreed by the Bishop of Rome, God's lexicographer. Bill's was an immaculate heart, unlike that of the engine of wickedness who now cast his shadow upon a page of Os.

"An ode is a poem you are supposed to sing," Bill read to Dave.

"Father Lachance is an asshole," said Dave. "They should give you a medal if you fuck a Protestant."

"What did you get for penance?"

"Nothing. I haven't even committed a sin yet. It's still at the planning stage."

"How do you spell 'fuck'?"

"Wake up, Bill. It's not in the dictionary."

"There's a lot of words in the dictionary," said Bill, his tone defensive.

"Not the good ones."

"There's some very excellent words in the dictionary. 'Ode' is an excellent word."

" 'Cunt' is an excellent word, and you won't find 'cunt' in there."

"How do you spell it?" asked Bill, flipping back out of the Os.

"Here comes Mom."

The car bounced into the churchyard, too fast, slewed to a halt in front of the steps.

"I'm still not used to these god *damn* power brakes," said Lucy Swan as the boys climbed in.

"Ten Hail Marys for 'damn'," said Dave. Bill took the back seat beside the groceries, careful not to lose his place in the dictionary. "Kukang," he pronounced. Lucy pulled away too fast, spraying gravel onto the church steps, bouncing out of the yard to the road. "Kupfernickel," articulated Bill. "I don't think it's in the Ks."

"Flog it, Mom," Dave urged his mother.

"You know, Dave, if you're going to wear those ascot scarves, you should learn how to tie them."

"A gentleman wears what he likes."

"As long as he knows how to tie it."

“Cunning,” read Bill, closing in.

“Tramp on it,” begged Dave. The car still smelled its new-car smell. Lucy pushed down lightly on the gas. They surged up a hill and out of Hudson, hurtled across railway tracks, and flew along the purple road to Como.

“Yeeee-haaaa!” yelled Dave as the car sank and rose on its oversoft springs.

“Female genital organs,” Bill declared in triumph. “What's genital, Mom?”

“Sorry?” said Lucy. But Bill had already struck off into the Gs on his own, flipping innocently towards that damp and glistening destiny that would one day, you may be sure, be plucking at his loins and sending him along in his brother's footsteps to that close cubicle where Father Lachance sat even now and fiddled sadly with his golden fringe.

“What did Bill say?” asked Lucy.

“Search me,” said Dave.

*

Here went the Swans, flashing along that windy road between tall maples, fences, glimpses of water to the left. They passed a large estate: fieldstone mansion sagging in the shade, windows shuttered, grass getting long on the lawn, lilies rotting in cool repose. A chain blocked the drive. Beyond the house, Lake of Two Mountains stretched away under a hard sun to a pair of bright blue hills.

“Are we going to take over Grampa's house?” asked Bill.

“The ancestral home of Rufus Swan, Esquire, K.C.,” pronounced Dave grandly, “the late deceased.”

“It's too big,” said Lucy.

A quarter-mile farther she slowed, turned in, and parked. A lawn dropped through a thin plantation of spruce to a tall white house, verandas flung into the shade of ancient trees. Above it all a red tin roof. Beyond the house a plunging lawn pitched downward into scrub. Past that, and down, there flowed the muscled current that emptied a million lakes, a continent, and slid on down to Montreal, downriver to Quebec, carrying, like every river, time itself, in one long act of measuring, draining a parade of days out of their mighty watershed and sweeping them into the past.

*

Into this past appeared the Swans, two hundred years before, with nothing nobler than a firm opinion on what to drink with fish. They came in arms, in the person of their antecedent Philip Swan, to help their country steal the continent of North America, once and for all, on the field of Quebec.

Philip Swan stood in a puddle waiting for the enemy to come and have a try at killing him. He thought, my dogs will have forgotten me when I get home. He remembered colours: a purple necklace that he had once taken from his mother's box and worn. He'd toddled out among his parents' friends, onto a green stone terrace behind the house. His father had scooped him up and kissed his face. "Excellent, Phil!" And now today it rained. He stood on that sad plain above a cliff, twenty-two years old, breeches ripped from the ascent, scarlet coat all caked with mud, sword resting on his shoulder. His teeth chattered. Grey clouds rubbed against the plain. He was soaked right through, could hardly move, when the French dragged their cannon onto that little crest and started to thin the British out with grape.

"Excellent!" cried Philip as the shot went whistling by his ears. A man fell, suddenly without a face, a pace behind him, and at the same instant Swan noticed that Wolfe had appeared in the midst of the line. "Fine day for a fight, sir!"

"You appear to be frozen, Mr. Swan."

"Excellent, sir! Fine day for it!" bawled Philip as his teeth chattered helplessly inside his ice-cold head. Another cannon shot.

"Have the men lie down, if you please, Mr. Swan," the general said, and off he walked as a load of shot came howling by, plucking at his hat.

"Very good, sir," shouted Philip. "Excellent!"

Finally the French charged: white uniforms legging it over the hill, soldiers of the line pelting down the slope in good order, but all mixed up, poor fellows, with that sorry mess of louts from the colony. The British waited, watching the irregular approach. At forty paces the officers' swords came down and the British volleyed. Blown to a bloody rag, the charge collapsed.

"Excellent," yelled Philip. "Advance!"

Somehow he managed to slog forward on legs that felt like iron, grateful not to disgrace himself, wondering if the trickle on his face was tears. He stepped on something that moved, a ruined soldier in the mud.

"Canterbury," the man said, just that one word from his punctured bit of face.

"Yes," Philip told him, "in Kent." He found a scrap of uniform, covered the soldier's throat, rose and advanced into loose fire. By now the French were falling back and the Scots on the right—more a ragtag of clans than a British regiment—had flung aside muskets and were bounding after the foe with claymores, taking heads. From a clump of yellow brush came a soundless fusillade of soft grey puffs, a magic trick appearing in the leaves. A tug at his sleeve made Philip look down.

"Oh, dash it all," he muttered at the mess that dangled in the rain below his elbow. He sat down hard on sodden ground, throwing up a splash.

"Sir!" cried his sergeant, rushing up. "They run!"

"Who run?" asked Philip.

"Sir, the enemy!"

"Excellent." He noticed that his teeth had ceased their chattering, and that he felt quite warm. "Go tell the general," and he fainted dead away.

That winter Philip Swan learned to clutch a bowl with one hand. He ate soup made from boiled onions and rancid game. Then he forgot to eat, then forgot his name. In January they dragged him down to the Hôtel-Dieu, to a tall grey room with a crucifix. The nuns wrapped this tossing bundle tight in linen sheets and expected it to die. "Excellent, Phil," he murmured when a cool hand touched his face.

By March he could speak whole sentences again and General Moncton came to visit. The nuns put Philip into a spotless shirt. They cleaned his scarlet coat so it glowed. The left sleeve had been cut and folded, sewn trimly shut. By contrast the general looked shabby, with bloodshot eyes and a grimy coat. "Ha," he said, hurrying into the room alone. "Well sir, Mr. Swan! I think you should get up!"

That spring the British held Quebec against a counterattack, took Montreal, and promptly fell in love, all of them, blown by a sudden amorous wind that came among them as they occupied the vanquished cities of the French. It was as if winter had worn them down and opened them to this strange, swift disease: that they love their enemy too well. Young officers wrote dreadful verse. Philip too. At a ball he spied a girl (not pretty at all, but lofty, bold) wedged between two bulldog dowagers. She wore a purple necklace. Philip rushed through the dancers and stood before her, feeling hot. He caught the necklace in his fingers and bent to kiss a stone. He felt his cheek brush against her mouth. When he raised his head, her blue eyes studied him. She turned her profile to him then, her long nose, declaring loudly to a guardian: "*Monsieur est parfaitement ivrogne.*" At this remark the older woman laughed, a high tough squeal, regarded Philip with a hanger-on's professional contempt, and said, "She say you are dronk." Philip kept his eyes on the girl. He stood there unsteadily, grasping a chairback for support.

"What a perfectly lovely nose," he announced to Françoise-Adélie Beaucourt de Saint-Victor, five-foot-ten of orphaned heiress, before he fell over and landed on his back.

Their courtship was too swift and dangerous even for those breakneck times. Philip ignored a coolness in the mess, married the girl without permission, scandalized the colony. Someone made a remark about French ladies and Philip struck him in the face. It would have come to pistols if Moncton had not heard. In the end Philip tore the buttons from his coat and flung them in the dirt.

The seigneuries of Beaucourt and Saint-Victor lay above Montreal, between the St. Lawrence and the Ottawa. They made a fair domain of hardwood maple, a dozen tenant farms, a scattering of mills. Françoise showed Philip how to ride like a maniac on forest trails. Their first child was born in a sled while they were gallivanting on a river, ignoring doctors, ignoring everyone. This was how they grew old: like children. Philip Swan was seventy-two when he caught a nasty kick.

"I shouldn't like to see her shot," he said of the mare, as he lay with his bandaged head in Françoise's lap. He remembered to tell his wife he loved her, and then died.

*

At Beaucourt the Swans passed from generation to generation; did not prosper; looted their inheritance instead. From time to time one would sell a farm or a little hill of trees. The proceeds might buy a thoroughbred or take him off to Baden, trailing a prodigal batch of Swans through Paris on the way. In the end their descendants owned only this capricious past, a few hundred acres, and a pair of harmless mansions on the Como shore: verandas spread like open arms, red tin roofs, lawns that ended at the river.

*

Bill watched Francine peg laundry to the line and reel it out. Out went the laundry, piece by piece, as Francine muttered away in a furious undertone. Every time she lifted some new garment to the line and sent it flying out, the hair under her arms shone darkly, suddenly revealed. Her bare legs were brown, and hairy too, the hair long enough to stir in the breeze.

"Her hairs are excellent," Bill commented silently.

From his place on the lawn below the kitchen porch he could also observe a dark, indeterminate area high up beneath Francine's dress where, he now supposed, a cunt was to be found.

For the last few days Bill had been trekking manfully about his dictionary, plodding his patient way back and forth between such unhelpful words as "organ" and "regeneration". Finally he was pretty sure he had run the thing to earth, cornered it there between Francine's legs. But he could get no closer than this, for the delicate and brittle laws that governed converse with a maid precluded Bill from asking her to let him take a look.

Weeding her way through her basketful of laundry, Francine struck a patch of Lucy's underwear. One by one these garments fluttered out. The panties troubled Bill. For if an organ of regeneration might be brought to bay inside Francine's own underwear, why not in Lucy's too? He decided to look up "mother". He would not ask Dave. Dave would drag out some scratchy word like "twat" and insist on making a diagram. Bill preferred to pursue the sense of words here, alone with his dictionary on this cloud of breathing grass, borne grandly along above that shoreline that was his by descent.

*

Rufus Swan, the lawyer, blew himself to bits atop a beaver dam. This was years after he had tried to drive the beavers off by sudden raids at night with flaming brands, years after he had dug that silly pit with stakes, years after he'd brought the alligator up from Florida to eat them. Now Rufus, this restless author of schemes, was dead, his house empty, a chain across the drive.

His end by dynamite surprised no one. It seemed fitting, not even remarkable, for a Swan to leave the world in particles flung outward. It was as if he had not died at all, but translated himself into another sphere. It had looked festive: a last large gesture by Rufus, like one of his famous parties on those verandas by the lake. His death was like that: something to amaze. Only Noel felt his father's death as a death.

> This is the last will and testament of me, Rufus Beaucourt Swan, of the village of Como, county of Vaudreuil, one of His Majesty's Counsel:
>
> 1. I hereby revoke any previous wills or testamentary depositions by me at any time heretofore made.
>
> 2. I name and declare my son, Noel Beaucourt Swan, barrister and solicitor, Esquire, to be the executor of this my will.
>
> 3. I give, devise and bequeath my entire estate, real and personal, to my son, Noel Beaucourt Swan, for his own use absolutely and for ever.
>
> In witness whereof I have hereunto set my hand at the City of Montreal.

Noel put the will aside. He sat at his father's desk. A warm night, windows open, sounds of light traffic drifting up from the Place d'Armes. Four antique boxes made of marbleboard were stacked beside the desk. These were a discovery. Rufus had kept personal letters and notes, scraps of his life, a running archive of his acts, planting exotic trees that never lived, keeping borzois, giving ladies boxes of fresh dates. Whenever he'd filled a carton, he'd locked it with a tiny lock, consigned it to the vault. Picking through it all at random, idly, Montreal prodding the night with distant honks or a sound of heels clicking through the square, Noel found a birthday card that Rufus had given him when he was three.

"To my darling boy, with love, from Papa."

"Dad," whispered Noel, "you never told me that," and he promptly left the office, didn't even lock the door, nodded at the porter, stepped into the Place d'Armes and headed for a drink.

"Imagine that," he said at the bar in Chez Delmo in Rue Notre-Dame. "Kept everything, even birthday cards, even mine."

"I liked that guy," asserted Duncan McIlraith.

"You bet," said Noel.

"Did you know you were crying?" asked Duncan.

"You bet."

*

Noel's firm was Swan and Swan. One Swan had now abruptly left, erased from practice as from life by a blast intended for beavers. The dynamite had exploded a good five minutes ahead of time, in fact while Rufus was trying to plant it among the twigs and mud. Noel had inherited the beavers, some maple woods, a portfolio of doubtful investments, the cartons, and Rufus's house. He could not afford to keep his father's house, although he would have liked to. He would have liked to move the cartons there, settle into those verandas, sunlit halls, staircases with landings the size of rooms. But if that house held something of Rufus, some evidence, then perhaps these cartons did too.

"Why did he keep all this?" wondered Lucy, as she and Noel waded into another crate of records.

"I don't know," said Noel. "He wasn't a very good lawyer. I guess he had a lot of spare time."

"Christ," breathed Lucy, sensing something larger, not

liking it. She shook her head and moved away. Their own back veranda was a wide porch behind square columns, view of the lake, plenty of rotting wicker and brave old terracotta tubs, filled this year with red and pink impatiens. Lucy rummaged among the blooms, flicking some away. Her movements were quick and precise, like the expressions that came and went on her face. She frowned at the half-dozen boxes, their little padlocks hanging open.

"They're not your letters, Noel," she said suddenly. "These are not your things." Noel looked, saw that her mouth was tight with disapproval.

"What's bugging you?"

"*This*." She included the archive in a sweep. "I think we should throw it out."

"It's just Dad's stuff."

"It's a whole *thing*," cried Lucy. "We should either turn it over to somebody, or burn it."

"Who would want it?"

"Then burn it."

Noel turned back to the boxes. "No way."

Into this tight silence drifted Bill, bearing with an excellent grace his personal burden of earnestness.

"Genital," he pronounced, marking his place with a finger. "Does everybody have a genital?"

"Yes," said Lucy, sourly examining one of Noel's boxes.

"Is it a cunt?"

"Oh, Bill," sighed Lucy.

"I'm afraid it's not a very polite word," said Noel.

"No," agreed Bill, "it is a vulgarism. It is a low expression."

"Do you think you should use it, then?"

"Well," reflected Bill, "I might as well."

Lucy waited until Bill left. "Maybe we should get a TV, Noel."

"I thought you didn't want one."

"Their reading is starting to embarrass the librarians."

"What, poetry?"

"And female anatomy. And steamy novels. And lately, some crazy book about food."

Noel shrugged. "There won't be anything worth watching on TV until the Coronation."

"I'd be happy if they'd watch cowboy movies."

*

"Dad," Dave interrupted Noel among the cartons, "is it a crime to make a plan?"

"Hand me that file there, will you, Dave?"

"Did you hear me, Dad?"

"Sorry?"

"Is it a crime to make a plan?"

"Well, if what you're planning is a crime, yes."

"What if what you're planning is only a sin?"

"I'm not a priest."

"Is fucking a sin? I mean, it's the joyous union of the male and the female, right?"

Noel was holding a clipping from the *Gazette*, had it bent to the light. "Did you know your Grampa once drove a cutter all the way from Como to Montreal along the river? There'd been a three-day blizzard and the trains weren't running. Your Grampa drove this cutter upriver, into the city, and tied the horse to a lamp post in Place d'Armes."

"You never listen to me."

"What?"

"Never *mind*," barked Dave, kicking one of the boxes as he stormed inside.

"There's even a picture," Noel called after him.

*

"Grampa *killed* himself," proclaimed Dave in a fury. "And now Dad's got that *junk*. I am coming into man's estate and my father is mired in the dark past of our family. Mired in the dark past," he repeated, in case Bill might have missed it.

"Not on purpose," Bill said quietly.

"Not on purpose *what*," demanded Dave, adding, as an afterthought, "you little turd."

"Grampa didn't kill himself on purpose."

"Oh shut up! How do you know? You total zit," Dave raged, his vehemencc against Noel unflagging when it came to abusing Bill.

"They don't let them bury you if you kill yourself."

"How do you know Holy Mother the Church didn't let them bury Grampa in consecrated ground because he paid for those new windows? Grampa paid for those new windows, and he paid for the man to come out from Montreal and put them in."

"Grampa did it for God," said Bill.

"Grampa did it to get his name in the church. So shut up."

"I'm not going to get mad at people when it's my turn to come into man's estate," Bill declared.

"How do you know about the currents of desire that seethe in the male? You have a pecker like a fly."

"I know how to read," Bill reminded him.

"Turd," Dave muttered viciously, flinging out of the room.

"You cried when they buried Grampa," Bill told him silently, after he'd left. "Mr. Swan bore a proud name and he bore it well," he quoted to the empty room. "Eternal rest grant unto him, oh Lord."

*

A machine began to moan down by the lake, rising to a loud hum, finally a whine. Then a saw bit into wood. Soon a smell of fresh sawdust, viscous and tangible, seethed up through the trees. Noel remembered the first time his father took him to swim at the sawdust beach at Charlie Hopkins's mill, there on the Como shore. He remembered Rufus's big hands holding him up. One hand made a platform for his stomach. He craned his head back and thrashed at the water. His father steadied him by spreading the other hand across his back, enfolding him in hands. "Do your strokes, Noel, the way I showed you."

This memory rode up on the heavy, sweet scent of sawn wood. He'd grown fast, shooting up by inches. He was only twelve when he swam across the lake, Rufus rowing at his side. He was already a strapping figure in his teens when the alligator arrived.

*

"I hate those boxes," said Dave from the house, watching his father's reverie. Noel intent on the veranda, poring over bits. "He's just looking for those stupid stories about Grampa. He's looking for the alligator story."

Lucy put a hand on Dave's shoulder. "Well, I guess they're *his* memories, aren't they?"

"But he's *our* father."

"We don't own him, Dave."

"He is supposed to tell me how to comport myself with the dignity of our station. I don't even know the right way to put in cuff links."

"I can help you with the cuff links."

"I hate that alligator."

*

They had picked it up at the station in Hudson, Noel and Rufus and Charlie. A rapt cortège followed the pickup as it banged through woods to the beaver pond. They stopped where the road disappeared into dark brown water, piled out to surround Charlie's truck. There was fresh mud on the dam and a few bright twigs, but no beaver in sight. Noel and another man tugged the crate out of the pickup and dropped it to the ground. They snipped the metal straps and crowbarred off the lid. A few men squished forward on the damp ground, leaned over the crate. The animal was five feet long, a light brownish-green, with a broad snout. His upper teeth protruded past his lower jaw. The jaws met in a sly, traitorous smile.

"*Alligator mississippiensis*," declared Rufus.

"Ain't that somethin', now," said Charlie.

Noel smacked at the crate with his crowbar. The boards let go and fell flat. Everyone drew back. The alligator turned his head, but otherwise stayed put. The men watched. Slowly the alligator closed his eyes, dragging a pair of thick lenses across them, then the lids. With his eyes shut, he moved no more.

"Their noses are valved," uttered Rufus suddenly. This remark was met with a stir of interest. Technical in nature, it appealed to the sturdy villagers. A general murmur of anticipation rose around the motionless reptile, and expectant faces turned to Rufus. Where such a datum had emerged, could others fail to follow? Rufus flushed.

"It's to keep the bloody water out," he added harshly.

"Sure," Charlie said to mollify him. "Now that *is* somethin'."

Forest sounds resumed. A kingfisher clattered across the beaver pond and a pair of squirrels squabbled overhead. A shiny beetle clambered onto the planks, made its way to the alligator's claw, and trudged steadily up the animal's leg. The men watched as the beetle proceeded stolidly along a trough in the alligator's armour and picked its way onto the head. Here it paused and flailed about with its antennae. Then it marched across a tightly shut eye, onto the long, flat nose, and settled down. The alligator remained still.

"Your turtle, now," said Charlie, breaking the hush, "your turtle'd snap that bug right up."

"Oh for heaven's sake," snorted Rufus. "Give the bloody thing a prod, will you?"

Noel took a long stick and tapped the alligator on the back. It sounded hollow, as if there were a gap between that tough hide and the animal inside. The alligator did not twitch.

"*Come* along," sneered Rufus, "give it a proper belt on the snout."

Noel circled gingerly, raised his stick, and delivered a clout to the nose. The alligator's eyes and jaws flew open. His tail lashed out and fired a plank into the watching men. They fell back with a howl. Hissing horribly, the alligator dug his claws into soft ground and shot into the pond. His thick tail whipped furiously about, thrashing that placid pool into a muddy foam. Finally he reached deep water and disappeared.

*

"Are we going to keep all Grampa's junk?"

"I wish you'd known him better," said Noel.

"Did he ever tell you about the mysteries of the male and the female?"

"I don't think so, Dave." He reached into one of the cartons. "This isn't junk, you know. You shouldn't call it junk."

"It's what Mom calls it."

"Does she?" asked Noel. He was surprised and, what surprised him more, hurt.

"Mom says that if there is going to be any discussion of the glory between the male and the female, it has to be with you."

"You bet," said Noel.

"You're not listening, Dad."

"Sorry, Dave. How's that again?"

"You should be telling me about the language of the eons that speaks from the male to the female, across the abyss of time, instead of mooning over this stuff."

"Is that what your mother calls it, mooning?"

"You never pay attention to me, Dad."

"This isn't mooning, Dave. It's my father."

"I'm supposed to have a father too."

"Do you remember when your Grampa trained that snapping turtle to swim behind his pontoon boat?"

"The only thing you never told me, Dad, is how the male is supposed to empty the vessel of his manhood into the female, which is something that would be very useful for a young male to know. Books don't tell you how, exactly. Like, how are you supposed to hold yourself on top of her? Do you just lie on her?"

Noel shoved some papers back into a box. "Let's wander over to your Grampa's. I should check the place."

"You should sell the place."

"Is that what your mother says?"

"I am your son," Dave insisted angrily. "I am in the thirteenth year of my age."

They followed a path beside the shore, came to Rufus's sagging boathouse, cut up across his failing lawn to a flight of steps alive with weeds. Dave pursued his goal of technical advice. Noel drifted away on the scent of water, earth, and leaves.

*

They had gone back to check on the alligator two days later. Noel remembered this now, coached by scraps of notes. This time they walked all the way in, a mile from the Como road. The track ran around Charlie Hopkins's fields, crossed the Canadian Pacific Railroad's main line from Montreal, and straggled into the Swans' wood. Deep maple forest, purple, echoey, cool against the skin. Blue jays flew ahead of them raising the alarm. Smooth grey trunks shot straight up to the vault of leaves. It was easy to walk in the dim transepts of the wood, where only ferns would grow. Rufus had once begun to revive a sugarbush in the wood, but in the end had abandoned the project.

"I cannot bear those pails," he'd said with loathing, ordered the spigots taken out, paid off the crew.

Now they walked without a word. Maples gave way to poplars and pine. It grew damp underfoot, and they came to the pond, lit by a hard, hot sun, a sudden white space in the forest. Insects blundered about, nursing on heat, swelling with that humid food of light until they crashed onto the surface, buzzed only fitfully, embraced at last that cool suck of liquid at their wings, and floated out of life.

They spotted him right away. He lay on the beaver dam, lordly, smiling his evil smile, sprawled among mud and sticks. No sign of beavers. Rufus frowned.

"The Assyrian came down like the wolf on the fold."

"I wonder if he ate their tails too," said Noel.

"*Come* along," snapped Rufus. "The bloody things aren't epicures."

He prowled the shore trying to suppress his triumph, smacking his stick into the mud and shooting vicious glances of approval at the dam. The alligator basked in his perfect furnace of mud and heat. Other than a single, cautionary glint, his eyes remained fast shut.

"Sleeping it off," crowed Rufus. "Ha!" he added, before he wrestled his lapsed dignity into control and led his legions back across the Rhine.

*

Ode to Floors
by William de Saint-Victor Swan, Esq.

This is a poem about our floors:
They smell superb like the outdoors:
Francine has waxed extremely good:
Now they smell nicer e'en than wood.

But anyway they are still wood:
You cannot make a floor from glass:
Because a person could fall down:
And get a cut upon his ass.

You can observe up Francine's dress:
When she hangs up our clothes:

But what it looks like right up top:
God only knows.

*

Nick Jackson ducked through the lilacs between her parents' property and the Swans'. She carried a thin metal tray painted with a design of flowers and friendly snakes. In the midst of this Eden, a vaguely rectangular, brownish object peeked from beneath a heavy napkin.

"Stop looking up Francine's dress," commanded Nick, setting her tray on the grass. "She knows you're looking. You come out every time." She tugged the napkin carefully into place.

"I'm trying to see her cunt," said Bill.

"You are too young to understand about love," Nick told him. She fiddled with the napkin. "I made Dave a special nut-bread."

"He values good nutrition," Bill recited.

"A woman needs to care for her man," said Nick. "The way to a man's heart is through his stomach. After that, they are totally in love with you for all of time."

*

"Dad," called Dave, "what kind of sperm count would somebody my age have?" The question began halfway up the stairs, thumped its way past the landing, and ended in the upstairs hall. "Would it be high enough to impregnate the female of the species?"

Noel was on a stepladder pushing open the trapdoor to the attic. He looked down.

"Sorry?"

Dave stopped at the ladder and looked up. "Sperm count, Dad. I'm planning to fuck Nick Jackson. I'm tired of hanging around waiting for a father to instruct a son. I'm just going to have to figure it out for myself. I want to conquer her as the male has conquered the female of the species from time immemorial."

"Sure," said Noel. "And it's the sperm count you want to know about?"

"I want to know if my sperm would be potent," Dave explained. "If it is, then Nick would quicken with child." Noel looked longingly at the attic. "I thought I should tell you about it," added Dave, "since I sprang from your loins."

"That's very thoughtful of you, Dave," conceded Noel. The smell of hot dust came down from the attic.

"I feel I must impregnate a female before I can experience manhood and its travails."

"Well," admitted Noel, "that would certainly be one way to draw a bead on the travails. But Nick is only thirteen, and I seem to recall that you're twelve."

"I am in the thirteenth year of my age. You think my sperm count would be too low?"

"It might be a hair on the low side, Dave, I don't really know. I just think you might want to get your sex life up and running a bit slower."

"You think I should start with cunnilingus?"

"Aw, shit," muttered Noel, and hoisted himself through the trap.

"He never listens to me," Dave complained as Noel disappeared.

"He keeps our family's history up there," said Bill. "It's Grampa's stuff."

"It's nuts," Dave ranted, "and it's an affront to the unity of this family."

"I just wonder what cunnilingus is, because it sounds like an excellent word."

"It's when you kiss a girl on the cunt," said Dave, staring up at the attic trap.

"I would never do that."

Dave shrugged. "That's because you don't have a sperm count."

"I don't need one," declared Bill.

"Shut up," said Dave. A sound of shuffling boxes came from the attic. "Come on," he summoned Bill. "I'll show you my plan."

They trooped off, out of one wing, down a step, into another. Bill was small, with a large round head and enormous eyes, light brown flecked with gold. He was a great starer, and his beautiful eyes fixed on things with sudden gravity.

Dave looked like his mother, had the same fastidious gestures, was neat, slim-boned, had eyes that were grey and quick. Lucy was short but Dave would be tall. Unlike Lucy, he was fiercely tidy. He loathed disorder. Lately he had acquired a rack for the ascot scarves he was steadily appropriating from Rufus's estate and Noel's closet. His library was carefully arranged: poetry with poetry; crime with crime; a special section for female anatomy and the general physiology of reproduction. Furniture, rugs, wall maps, bulletin boards, the notices on the boards: all obeyed a rule of squared-off harmony imposed by him whose name was boldly lettered on the bedroom door: David Beaucourt Swan, Esq. A tidy desk waited by a window. A stoneware jar held his armament of pens. An enormous Bostitch stapler guarded the desk with ferocity.

Dave opened a filing cabinet, withdrew a folded paper, opened it on the bed. It was a hydrographic chart of the

Lake of Two Mountains, brightened by a series of clean, red boxes that had been drawn along the shore.

"Here's our house," said Dave, "and here's Nick's. And here's the sawmill."

"It's a secret map," said Bill appreciatively.

"Every day Nick goes down to the sawdust pile to swim." Dave tapped the paper to show where the sawdust was, between the sawmill and the lake. "She arrives between fourteen hundred hours and fifteen hundred hours."

"Maybe she'll bring a nutritious food."

"On D-Day, I will approach the target zone at fourteen-thirty hours," Dave continued. "Nick should be in the water by then. I will do a cannonball off the seawall and land beside her. Nick hates to get splashed."

"She'll call you a dink."

Dave tapped the map. "If she doesn't get out of the water right away, I'll do another cannonball. Finally she'll get out."

"Then she'll dig a hole in the sawdust to get warm."

Dave pushed aside the chart and unfolded a neat drawing on graph paper. The mill's outline was boldly drawn, its walls hatched in tight little strokes of rusty red. A huge pile of buff-coloured sawdust rose beside the mill. There was a girl, shown standing knee-deep in the pile, sex indicated by a pair of meticulous bumps on her chest.

"She'll dig a hole in the sawdust to get warm," said Dave. He pointed to another drawing. This one had no bumps. Instead it had a sticklike penis. "I will dig a hole beside her."

"She might call you a shit-brain."

"The deeper you dig in the sawdust pile," said Dave, "the hotter it gets. I will challenge Nick to see who can stand the deepest hole. The vanquished must grant the victor's request."

"A woman needs to care for her man," Bill agreed.

"I will take her under the sawmill and fuck her." Dave studied the chart.

"We're not allowed in there."

"That's when Nick kisses her cherry goodbye."

"Mom will never let you go under the mill."

"The female of the species longs for conquest."

"I seem to recall that you are only twelve."

"Shut up, Bill."

*

"Dave is going to fuck Nick Jackson, Mom."

"Don't say 'fuck', Bill."

"He's going to take her under the sawmill. She will be vanquished, and will have to kiss her cherry goodbye."

"Bill," said Lucy, standing on her tiptoes and peering into a cupboard, "did you see those chocolates?"

"Dave threw them out."

Lucy looked at her son. "He what?"

"He said they were full of shit."

"Don't say 'shit', Bill. It's not nice."

"Dad says 'shit'."

"He doesn't mean it." Lucy looked back into the cupboard.

"He threw them in the lake," Bill told her again. "They are nothing but refined sugar and myriad toxins."

"Oh God," groaned Lucy. "That little shit."

"Hey!"

"I don't have anything for dessert."

"A chocolate is not really for dessert. It's a digestive."

"God *damn*."

"There are a lot of bad words in this family."

"I know, Bill," said Lucy. She sounded tired.

"Sometimes I don't know why you bother being a mother. You could be a lawyer like Dad. You are a trained lawyer."

"I'm a trained mother, too."

"But you don't get your own office."

"I could be an axe-murderer, I suppose."

"You still wouldn't get your own office."

"Good point," said Lucy. She opened the fridge and looked in. "There's some of that nut-bread that Nick made."

"It's like eating boards."

"I could heat it up and put ice cream on it."

"You could pour intoxicating spirits on it and light it and have a footman carry it in on a silver tray," said Bill. "Or you could stuff it with hummingbirds' tongues. Roman emperors liked to have things stuffed with hummingbird tongues. It might be good."

Lucy looked at him. "Bit bloodthirsty, aren't we?"

"Not for the mightiest Roman of them all."

*

Noel burrowed on into carton after carton, following his father back to that pond with its smell of mud, its smell of the waterproofing grease that Rufus plastered on his boots.

"We'll have to shoot the bugger," Rufus said, tramping through the woods on their way to the pond. "His job's done. Can't have him shuffling off after the cows."

They left the maple grove and followed a trail that wound through thinning bush. Where the ground began to dampen, they met an unexpected obstacle. A tree had been newly felled, its smaller branches stripped away. Broad teethmarks were plainly visible on the stump. Rufus reddened, climbed slowly over the tree, continued to the shore. The alligator sprawled as before, only now there were fresh twigs and branches planted in the earthwork of the dam, some of them right alongside the slumbering reptile. Rufus breathed heavily through his nose. His lips were tight. A narrow gleam of eye appeared in that long, green-brown head, watched a moment, disappeared.

"Must be a new lot that's moved in," Rufus pronounced in the face of this fresh evidence. "Our friend will get to them as soon as he's slept off that last lot."

"Maybe he's sick," said Noel. "Maybe he doesn't know they're food. Maybe they're the same beavers."

Rufus smothered with a glance these tiny flames of speculation, turned, and abandoned the beavers to their certain fate.

*

Bill sat with Margaret Curry in a crooked yellow sunroom, an old and spavined structure that remained attached to the Currys' renovated house. This sunroom's survival seemed miraculous, for Gordon Curry, Margaret's father, dearly loved a wrecking bar.

Still, here it was, colonized by Bill and Margaret and Margaret's cat, a slovenly creature the size of a spaniel who went by the name of Curly. Margaret crouched over the slumped form of Curly, dabbing livid specks of nail polish onto the tips of his ears. Curly twitched his ears and slid a look of loathing Margaret's way, but otherwise remained as inert as a sack of rocks.

"Dave always tells me to shut up," said Bill, "because he gets mad at Dad. Dad is mired in the history of our family." Margaret studied Curly, her face beatific and remote, loaded with that innocence that squashes bugs.

"I am an angel," she said to Bill, "but Curly is *not* an angel cat."

"But he never gets mad at you."

"He loves me," she affirmed.

"In sickness and in health," said Bill.

*

"Did Dave like my nut-bread, Mrs. Swan?"

"It was very nice of you, Nick."

"I can never find that man anywhere." Nick followed Lucy through the house. They crossed the veranda and went down to the lawn. Nick watched as Lucy began to prowl about among some roses with her enormous secateurs.

"I worry about Dave's diet, Mrs. Swan."

"So does he," said Lucy.

Nick found a weeding fork. She made a few desultory stabs into the grass and then began to pounce upon dandelions with a ferocity that left whole patches of lawn looking as if they had been weeded by artillery. "I worry that he doesn't get essential foods," she confessed, surveying her work with a troubled expression.

"Oh yes?"

"I don't want to hurt your feelings, Mrs. Swan."

"If you slide that fork down along the tap root, those dandelions will come out quite easily, Nick."

"Dave is a man, and he needs a full range of proper foodstuffs," Nick reported, pushing the fork down carefully, wiggling it experimentally.

"He throws out a pretty full range as it is," said Lucy, watching Nick manœuvre a foot-long root from the grass. "That's the way!"

"Gee," said Nick, admiring the root. And later, "Do you think Dave would like a bread with beans in it? It's supposed to be very healthy."

"You can always try. God knows, if he doesn't like it, it won't be around for long."

"But don't you just love that in a man, Mrs. Swan? I mean, their boldness?"

"Easy on the lawn, Nick."

*

"She's still out there," said Bill, peering from the upper veranda.

"Don't let her see you," hissed Dave.

"She's helping Mom. She's weeding the dandelions."

"She should just feed them some of that nut-bread."

"She made it so you would get proper nutrients and have a balanced diet."

"The only diet I want from that broad is pussy juice."

"Well, that sounds disgusting."

"Shut up, Bill."

*

"Noel!"

Lucy peered up at the attic. Brown dust hung in the hot air. She heard her husband moving in the darkness, out of sight.

"Noel?"

"Luce?" Noel's lopsided smile appeared in the dark square of the trap. "Hey."

"Hey yourself," said Lucy. She climbed up the ladder and perched at the top. "You're not trying to read up here, are you?"

"I've rigged a pretty good light."

Lucy nodded. "Your dad's stuff?"

"There's all kinds of incredible stuff."

"You've been at it a week."

"I feel close to Dad."

"Your dad wasn't close to anybody, Noel."

Noel grinned. Lucy took his hand. It was dirty with smudged dust, hatched with paper cuts. "That little shit has been throwing out food again."

"Dave? Stop feeding him."

Lucy frowned. "Do you think?"

"It might sharpen his sense of food as a valuable commodity."

"Kind of draconian," said Lucy.

"That's what I like about it," answered Noel.

Lucy put her other hand over his. "I hate to ask this. How long are you planning to stay away from the office?"

"Don't know," responded Noel. He looked back into the dusty attic. "I want to straighten out a few more boxes." He grinned at Lucy, kissed her hand, and crawled away into the dark.

*

Margaret sat on a footstool in her underwear, her dress discarded at her side. Curly strolled into the room, swept a look of disgust at Margaret, stretched, and sagged onto the dress. Margaret gazed sweetly at the cat, reached down, and whipped her dress out from beneath him, sending the astonished Curly tumbling onto his back.

"Naughty," she pronounced. "Naughty." She dropped the dress back onto the floor. Curly looked at her with yellow eyes, licked his right paw twice, and took himself into a corner from which he surveyed the children with tranquil hatred. Margaret sat very straight on the stool and clasped her arms behind her. This position forced the narrow bones of her scapulae to stand out in a pair of sharp triangles. Bill examined them intently.

"There are no feathers."

"They are my wings," said Margaret placidly. "Father said so."

"Does it hurt?"

"No. I am an angel."

Margaret smelled of Yardley soap. Bill thought her perfect. Peach hairs grew on her back. In that yellow room her skin was yellow too, with green from the grass outside. Green and yellow and, of course, blue.

"You are excellent," Bill told her.

"I am an angel."

"Can you cook?"

"Yes. I am an angel."

"Maybe if you loved a man you would cook him nutritious food."

"The man would barbecue," said Margaret flatly. "He would bring out the coals for the barbecue and the barbecue starter."

"Who would take care of *him*?"

"He would love me 'cause I am his little angel."

*

"Bugger must be *dead*," said Rufus. The reptile lay as before, a muddy hide draped along the dam. But instead of evidence of a routed enemy, they found signs of the beavers' ceaseless work. Nothing seemed to have been interrupted. There were more twigs on the dam, planted firmly into place beside that effigy of sleep. They stalked around the pond for an hour, examining the shore for sign of a scuffle.

"Not a bloody *hair*," growled Rufus. He glared at the motionless beast. "Climb out on the dam, there, and give that blasted handbag a whack."

"I don't know, Dad."

"Use a stick," said Rufus generously.

Noel found a long stick and made his way round to one end of the dam. The alligator remained locked in apparent torpor, or, Noel prayed, death. He felt his way onto the dam, placing his feet with care. The muddy structure was soft and springy, but its tough construction held. Flies buzzed around the alligator's nose. A string of bright green slime trailed from a huge tooth. Noel crept out farther on the dam, closing to about ten feet from the alligator. He leaned forward, reached out with his stick, and tapped the animal's nose. Nothing.

"Fetch it a good clout," called Rufus. Noel tapped again. This time the alligator's jaws flew open. There came an awful, choking roar, and Noel felt a blast of nauseating breath. He stumbled back, dropping his stick, tripping and sitting down hard on mud and twigs. The alligator roared again. Noel scrambled backwards on hands and feet. The alligator made a sudden rush, bursting forward a yard. Noel threw himself off the dam. He landed in waist-deep water. The alligator slid from the dam like a serpent, vanishing into the brown water with a sound like a hiss. Noel flailed wildly at the surface and thrashed ashore. He galloped away from the water, stopping to turn only when he was a dozen yards into the trees.

"Not dead, then," observed Rufus drily.

*

Noel's abandonment of his practice was never declared, but it was inexorable. Lucy tried at first to wrest an admission from him, some acknowledgement. Finally her assaults grew blunt on Noel's wordlessness. She began to accept that she was helpless to move him. Noel drifted away into an accretion of days. His father's archive pulled him irresistibly. His partners began to understand that he would not return.

In the Place d'Armes they commenced the business of removing him. Every few weeks Noel would trail in on the mid-morning train, sign a stack of documents prepared for him, poke around the office with a distracted air, and finally wander down Rue Notre-Dame to Chez Delmo.

"What's happened to all that stuff of your dad's?" Duncan McIlraith asked him on one of the last of these visits, as they loitered into their third bottle of wine.

Noel smiled.

"I'm learning a lot."

*

Ode to Margaret
by William de Saint-Victor Swan, Esq.

I dont think Margaret has a cunt:
I think that she has wings instead:
I hope they dont grow out too fast:
And flop around o'er her head.

I hope the wings dont make her bleed:
They have to grow right through your skin:
I guess it would be e'en worse:
If they grew in.

I hope she doesnt fly away:
An angel can fly o'er a tree:
I think people should stay at home:
Like me.

*

Dawn. The squeak of metal pins in oarlocks, *scree-screek, scree-screek*. Soon the boats appeared, drawing towards Como from the Oka shore. Two pairs of oars to the boat, the Indians pulled across in easy sweeps. By a quarter to seven they were dragging their boats onto the sawdust beach. By seven the saws were going.

Jesus Morris, a lordly and taciturn Mohawk chief, Charlie's sawyer, would flick his eye at a log as it rumbled up the slide, decide in that single glance what boards the log would yield, and run it straight through his saw without a pause. First a strip of slab was sheared from its side. The carriage shot back again for another pass, and another, until the log was squared and ready to deliver the shining planks decreed by Jesus Morris.

Lumber went into a shed. Slab was stacked in the yard by Hugh and Archie, also Mohawks. Other Indians came and went, floating from job to job, oiling machinery, mending chain, hauling logs by boat in summer, by horse in winter. Still, the place ran at a loss. Even in that brave day, when a fresh reign seemed to cast its light into the rivers of the dominion, Charlie's mill was not so much a business as an efflorescence of the river itself, a place for smells and people, horses and sawn wood.

"I didn't know angels were girls," Bill confided sadly to Charlie when he finally tracked the old man down.

"Well, now," said Charlie.

"Do their wings grow out like tits?"

"Well, now."

Only the summer before, Charlie had identified a strange bird that appeared on a boom of logs. "That'd be a cormorant," Charlie had remarked with perfect omniscience. It was a huge bird, sooty black. The boom of logs where it rested lay tethered inshore. Flat-footed and sullen, the bird regarded them with a fierce eye. "Nature, eh?" said Charlie. "Ain't she somethin'?"

Behind Bill's solemn countenance there lived a Borgia. Words were the treasure that he chased through his personal Italy of books. He found them excellent. And so when Charlie recognized a cormorant, unfurling its black, proud, wicked name into that summer's day, the chair of ornithology was his for good. Including angels.

"Mothers have tits, but no wings."

"Well, now." Charlie gazed imploringly at the mill, praying for Jesus Morris to emerge from the sawyer's booth.

"The female of the species," Bill rehearsed, "longs for conquest. So I don't know how come they're angels."

"Well," said Charlie, blundering about for any exit, "a woman, now; you never know with a woman."

*

"D-Day," announced Dave. His map was tacked to the bulletin board. Coloured pins marked tactical locations.

"Maybe Nick won't go swimming today," said Bill.

"Wake up," said Dave, "it's about a hundred degrees."

"Maybe Colonel Jackson will go with her."

"That old fart won't budge from his pansy bed all day."

"Maybe Nick won't let you fuck her. You never know with a woman."

"Get real, Bill. The female longs for sexual union with the male of the species. It's how they get spermatozoa."

"They might not want it."

"The erectile tissues of the female genitalia make them want it. It's why they have vestibular bulbs and a clitoris."

"Nick is only thirteen."

"Bill, that broad is so desperate to get laid she can hardly breathe."

"She was breathing okay yesterday."

"If you tell anybody I'll kill you."

"Everybody knows. You already told them."

"They don't know the details."

"You're a strange kid, Dave."

"*I'm* strange? Bill, I don't even know what *planet* you come from."

"Earth."

*

Noel kept to the attic. There were other rooms he could have used, but he decided to keep the archive in the cramped space beneath the roof. "That's where we put it when we got it, let's leave it there," he said. Lucy understood that Noel's choice had nothing to do with convenience. He liked being up there, that was all. His trips into Montreal grew more infrequent. He withdrew into the pages of his father's archive.

Although nothing had prepared Lucy for this retreat, she began to understand as she scoured their past for clues that there had been something tenuous in their life. Noel, she recognized, had been disposed to withdraw. Gentle, loyal, massively forgetful; affectionate for all of that. He would allow his sons to badger him down to the lake. There they would clamber onto his shoulders, their patient ox, urging him into deep water, howling as the water rose around their walking mountain.

You always put up with that, Lucy said to herself on one of her long, ransacking trips through their past.

She thought, we were not talkers.

Their disputes had been silent ones, settled by a kind of wordless shifting that occupied a few days, at most a week. By the time they were through there was a new strand in the web of custom, a new canon. No one needed to proclaim it.

That's why we can't talk now. We never did.

Lucy was tiny compared to Noel, but tougher. She walked more firmly and her gestures had more purpose. Her shining hair and pale skin were her most feminine features. Her eyes were too steady to be beautiful, her lips too tight.

"Am I alone in this?" she asked Noel one afternoon, heaving her courage into place. They were on the long back lawn, a swoop of weedy grass. Noel was poking in a puzzled way at the sagging frame of a swing. His tool box was on the grass. Lucy had been rooting intruders out of the dahlias, and suddenly she just sat back on the grass and asked him the question. Noel was silent for a minute.

"No," he replied at last, "you're not."

"I feel like it."

"I think I could start a small business," he said, not looking at her, tentatively shoving at one of the narrow benches, setting it to swing. "Something outdoors."

"Fixing swings?"

Noel shrugged. "We're okay for money."

"We're *not*," contended Lucy vehemently. "We have *some*, Noel, a little. But we run through money so fast."

"We have Dad's estate."

Lucy shook her head and pulled off her gardening gloves. "What's going on, Noel? People are talking about us, you know."

"I didn't think you cared about that."

"Of course I care about it. We live in a village full of people we know."

"I couldn't breathe in that office."

"You never told me."

"I know."

Lucy tossed her gloves onto the grass. She gazed through the trees to the bright lake. A squadron of tiny sailboats battled each other around a buoy that marked the yacht club's training course. The children's orange life-jackets blazed in white sunlight as one by one each frantic skipper rounded the buoy, ducked beneath the boom, and darted away on the new tack, full of purpose.

*

Dave and Bill crept through brush. To their left they could see a terrace of the Jacksons' lawn. A sketching party perched on canvas chairs and scratched away at views of the sagging mill. Clementine Jackson held sway, puffing along through the afternoon in a voice as familiar as wind itself.

"I never get tired of it," she pronounced, waving a pencil at the mill. "*Never.*"

"Quite right," chimed one of the sketchers, "the volumes are smashing. Those surface textures are positively edible."

Clementine frowned.

"So dilapidated," another offered.

"So *quaint*," corrected Clementine, who reserved to herself the right to supply whatever modifiers might be needed to describe the mill. "Bud is going to buy it."

"Ah," said the first lady. "To preserve it?"

"To knock it into the lake, I should think," said Clementine cheerfully, and a brief silence visited the little group.

"Mrs. Jackson will see you, Dave," whispered Bill.

"Shut up, Bill. If Mrs. Jackson hears us I'll have your guts for garters."

"You heard Grampa say that."

"Shut up."

They entered an alley beside the forge. An open door poured out a smell of cold iron and rust, of axle grease and ashes. Opposite, Charlie's office was locked with a padlock, its windows cloaked in abandoned webs. A special world inhabited this umbral region between sheds. Shadflies thronged the weathered boards or lashed about in spiders' webs. A peculiar species of striped beetle plodded morosely about, and shining brown-red woodbugs darted into cracks. Beyond, sunlight poured into the mill yard. Heat struck the sawdust-packed dirt and filled the air with a pungent smell.

"Mrs. Jackson will see you."

"Piss on Mrs. Jackson."

"They will see you if you try to fuck Nick."

"Not if I go around by the slab."

Charlie's mill lay between them and the lake. Stacked slab was piled beside it on the right. The huge sawdust pile and sawdust beach were out of sight beyond the mill.

"Mrs. Jackson will be mad if she knows you are going to ejaculate Nick."

"Darling, there you are!" Clementine's voice sailed over the trees. Nick came down the steps to the lower lawn. "Going for a bathe, Nicola?" her mother hooted.

"I'm going for a swim," said Nick in her flat voice.

"Shall I come along?" one of the party trilled. "I'll do a little *jeu d'esprit* of you, shall I?"

"That old shitbag," muttered Dave.

"No," said Nick, and she ducked through a gate into the mill yard.

"Bingo," breathed Dave as she disappeared from sight. For a moment the forge blocked their view, then Nick reappeared, walking around the left side of the mill towards the beach. Dave waited until she disappeared.

"Beat it," he hissed at Bill, and ran for the nearest stack of slab.

*

Charlie's seawall had been dragged together over decades and had spent as long subsiding into ruin. Loosened by years of spring ice, its boulders now descended by inches into the sluggish current. Behind the mill they collapsed for good, and sank from sight beneath a spongy beach of sawdust and bark and sodden chips. Here the Indians dragged up their boats, and here was the private riviera of Jacksons and of Swans.

Nick dropped her towel on a log, sat, stretched her tanned legs. She seemed to be admiring them, turning them this way and that. Finally she ran into the water, dove, and swam out a few strokes. The submerged remnant of a stone pier lay offshore. When she reached it she put down a foot and found the stones. She stood, and her shoulders cleared the water. Hidden by slab, Dave watched. Suddenly he felt silly, a boy with skinny legs and a saggy bathing suit.

"Hey," Nick shouted from the water, "what are you waiting for?" Dave froze. Bill, he thought. That little turd.

"Hey, male of the species," Nick called, "isn't this where I get raped?" Dave emerged from his hiding-place.

"Hi."

"Oh, brother," said Nick when Dave swam out with a silly grin. She was an inch taller than Dave, with the same skinny build. Her blonde hair was plastered against her narrow face. "I thought this was supposed to be pussy time."

Dave blushed. "I'll kill that kid if he told you."

"You're acting pretty stunned, Dave," she said in a level voice. "It's okay for a man and a woman to love each other, you know. People do fall in love. People do make nut-bread for their loved ones. You don't have to be such a hick, Dave. You're supposed to kiss me first."

"I don't feel like it."

"Aren't you horny?" demanded Nick, reaching a hand under water and touching his crotch.

"Hey!" cried Dave, stumbling off the sunken stones and taking in a mouthful of water.

"David Swan," said Nick disgustedly, "you are a dink," and she stroked away from the rocks and swam to shore.

"You're in big trouble, Dave," she told him when he joined her. They climbed to the top of the sawdust pile, scooping the hot flakes onto their wet legs. "Your dad quit."

"I don't know if he quit," said Dave. "He's, like, an owner."

"What are you guys going to do?"

"I think we have some money."

"What if you have to move?"

"I would hate that," he admitted.

As if they had reached a conclusion, some pact, they started to dig down into the sawdust. Soon they had scooped out a wide cavity. At the bottom the sawdust was damp and warm. They dug deeper. Their arms and legs were caked with wet sawdust and sawdust clung to their hair. Now the hole was a yard deep. The sawdust floor was hot. They stood side by side, grimacing at each other. Dave reached out and drew an armload of sawdust into the cavity. Nick did the same. Soon they were packed in with sawdust piled to their waists. They looked at each other and giggled at their recklessness.

"It's getting hot," confessed Nick.

"Yeah," Dave agreed.

"Yeah."

They were sweating. There was no shade on the pile and the sun burned. Against their buried feet rose waves of damp and painful heat, out of the mysterious furnace at the deep centre of compacted chips. Nick took a tentative swipe at the sawdust that held them in place. Dave seized the signal and soon they were flinging sawdust aside and laughing crazily. When they were free they lay side by side, coated with sawdust, sawdust inside their bathing suits.

"I have sawdust on my tits," said Nick.

"Yeah," said Dave.

A cool smell of water blew off the lake. Nick's hand strayed to Dave's and plucked at his fingers. His hand remained limp but he did not draw it away. She brushed the sawdust from his stomach.

"Dave," she leaned over, breathing the words into his face. "Do they, like, teach you guys about sex?"

"What, the nuns?"

"Your folks."

"Oh sure," he said, suddenly depressed. "We can talk about anything at our place."

"I could show you a lot," suggested Nick.

"We would have to make an assignation." He sounded doubtful.

"Do you love me, Dave?"

"You walk in beauty," he told her, "like the night."

*

"Bless me, Father, for I have sinned. It is two weeks since my last confession. I had to throw out some food. It had guar gum in it, and I don't think that's good for the human physical system, although I'm not sure and that's why I'm confessing it. Just in case. I think it's better to be straight with God."

"Pray to the Blessed Virgin, my son."

"Sure."

"She will guide you if you pray with a contrite heart."

"Okay."

"Is there another thing, my son?"

"Would touching a girl's tits be impurity if you were trying to clean off the sawdust?" Dave could see the priest turn his head a fraction, trying to sneak a sideways glance through the grate. He covered his face with his hands.

"To touch a woman with an impure thought, this is a mortal sin."

"She's Protestant, Father."

"Say the rosary five times. Pray to Our Lady. Come and see me after mass."

"Fuck you," muttered Dave as he left the church.

*

"Your beaver, now; your beaver is a nocturnal creature," Charlie had told them that time they went in at night, Rufus and Noel and Charlie, in Charlie's truck. "What your beaver is on the lookout for," continued Charlie, "is barks. He loves certain barks. The poplar is a bark he loves."

"He has eaten every poplar I own," scowled Rufus.

"He'll do that," said Charlie, nodding his head. "He'll eat a bark until there is no more of that bark left. What this means, and this is the bad part, is that there won't be any of that tree left, either. Once a beaver sets his heart on a bark, the tree that bears that bark is staring its Maker right in the face. The grim reaper waits for that there tree with a scythe made out of beaver teeth."

"For heaven's sake," growled Rufus, and Charlie said no more.

They parked and went in on foot. Stripes of moonlight lit their way. Rufus wore enormous rubber boots and carried a long flashlight. He approached loudly along the road, sweeping the woods with his powerful beam.

"Can't have the fellow stealing up behind us, eh?" he declared fiercely. Charlie and Noel followed carefully. They emerged at the pond with the moon behind them. An armload of thin, metallic light lay on the water. They studied the tangle of twigs and mud, the crenellated architecture of the dam, but the alligator was not there.

Finally a black shape coasted into the moonlight.

"Beaver," said Charlie.

"*Castor canadensis*," confirmed Rufus, "the rodent." The dark shape glided out of the moonlight and vanished into darkness. They waited while the beaver sloshed noisily ashore and trundled away from the water's edge. Next they heard a gnawing sound. A few minutes more and there came a sharp cracking, and a thump. A tree had fallen in the forest. Shortly after, they heard dragging noises. Soon the beaver reappeared in the moonlight, towing a leafy branch. He coasted across the pond, hauled his trophy onto the dam, and set to stripping bark.

"Where is that *bloody* lizard?" snarled Rufus. He shone his flashlight into shadows, probing along the shore. A pair of bright reflections jumped out of the darkness. The alligator was squashed in among fallen branches. His head was turned to face them and his eyes glowed murderously in the electric light.

"Good lad," breathed Rufus as the alligator stirred. It inched forward like a mechanism, notch by notch, until it slid onto the silver pond and drifted out. The beaver on the dam stopped eating. He watched the little trail of bumps that floated purposefully across the shining water, dragging a thread of ripple in its wake. As it neared the dam, he scrambled off, delivered a resounding blow to the surface with his strong, flat tail, and disappeared. Other smacks replied from dark corners of the pond, then silence. The alligator prowled about on the surface, gliding here and there, before he gave up the search and returned to shore. Rufus turned away in disgust. They left the reptile as before, squatting in shoreside mud while night birds called and a rasping noise of frogs broke out around the pond.

*

Bill learned much about angels, tracking them through the chaotic shelves of Hudson's pink stone library. Avid in research, he followed the rustle of wings from a useless, rotting volume of nineteenth-century theology, through several encyclopaedias, and into poets great and small.

He learned that angels fought wars, surging through heaven in their tens of thousands and sending each other tumbling through smoking clefts of time to lakes of fire. He learned that angels had faces of red glass and seraphs each three pairs of wings: one to hide their faces, one for hovering, one to wrap their seraphic feet from sight.

He learned that they could be men, but that in a fight the women angels were as quick to snatch a sword. They might be small and naked. These were the cherubim, who played on ceilings or in beds where vast round women lay carnally displayed. All angels bred like flies.

"There are 49 million angels," he told Margaret in their yellow room on a day that rained. The rain added a lick of blue and a luscious, ochred grey to Bill's bare torso. He sat very straight, arms clasped behind his back, while Margaret inspected his projecting shoulder blades.

"You're not an angel," she told him then. "Those are just bones."

"They might grow later."

"Take off your pants," instructed Margaret. "I want

to see your pee-pee."

Bill stepped promptly out of his short pants and slid his underwear to his knees.

"That's a very stupid pee-pee," Margaret judged.

"It's a penis," Bill corrected her.

"It will fall off when you're ten."

"Dave is in the thirteenth year of his age, and he still has one."

"It's a different one," said Margaret. "This one will fall off."

*

"I bought a Caterpillar," Noel declared quite suddenly.

"A what?"

"You know, a bulldozer. To do some work."

Lucy opened the fridge, closed it. "I guess there's no chance you're kidding."

"I thought you wanted me to work."

"Well that's fine, then," Lucy said tightly. "Now we have a bulldozer."

"I thought I might put a road into the sugar bush, and sell a lot or two," Noel said. It sounded like an apology.

"And you can drive a bulldozer, can you?"

"It can't be that hard."

"It's a god damn marsh in there."

"Yes," he answered thoughtfully. "I'd have to get rid of the beavers."

"You may have to get rid of *me*." The door slammed behind her.

*

"Really," said Dave, "it's a bit thick."

Night. They lay in their pyjamas on a chaise on the upper veranda, a cluttered porch whose entrance was through Bill's bedroom. Bill lay with his head against Dave's shoulder. Around the house stirred masses of unseen foliage. The lake slid smoothly by beyond trees, beyond the stain of scent that marked the mill, sliding its liquid body through the channels of the river lake.

"Will we have to move?"

"I don't know," acknowledged Dave.

"You'll have to marry Nick if you want to take her with us."

"I know," said Dave, "but only if we have to move."

"Would Mrs. Jackson let you marry her?"

"Marriage is a sacrament. It's a holy rite of Holy Mother the Church. Mrs. Jackson is not even a Catholic. If she tried to stop me the Pope would cast her soul into the torment of hell where it would languish with the other souls of the damned until Christ should come to raise the living and the dead."

"Then what?" asked Bill.

"Then we would have to see."

*

Beside Charlie's slab yard lay the strip of land that belonged to Gordon Curry, Margaret's father, a wealthy haberdasher. Although this property now met the shore, it had once been stranded at the road. Curry's attempts to buy a right-of-way had met with various rebuffs, for people tended to detest him. But somehow he had managed, and his property now ran down to the shore alongside that of a pair of maiden sisters named Lofft, who had sworn to sow their land with salt before an inch would pass to a jumped-up peddler like Gordon Curry. It was Curry's son Ian, Margaret's older brother, who now led a raiding party onto the Lofft beach.

A few collapsing groins ran into the shallows here, and a pen had been formed by dragging the remnants into a rough rectangle. Within this enclosure a morose population of ducks paddled toward the end that attends us all.

"We'll hit them with rocks," decided Ian.

"Get real," said Dave. "I thought you were bringing a net."

"Ducks are ungainly," declared Bill.

"Shut up, you little fart," snapped Ian.

"Don't call my brother a fart," said Dave.

"Why does he have to bring that stupid knapsack?"

"Leave him alone."

They arrived at a chicken-wire fence that sagged from its posts. A sign warned trespassers off.

"Margaret," barked Ian to his sister, "go get Dad's fishing net." Margaret hesitated, fearing to be left out, and smiled imploringly. "If you don't get that net right now," said Ian, "I'll mash you into guts."

"You shouldn't bully a girl," said Dave as Margaret hurried off.

"Shut up, Swan," snarled Ian, clenching his fists.

"Go fuck yourself," Dave told him. They pushed aside the wire and slipped through. Ducks were starting to quack nervously and crowd towards the far side of their enclosure.

"I am the expedition leader," Ian claimed.

"Bullshit," Dave told him.

"You want to get pounded?" demanded Ian. He was thirteen and had an inch of height on Dave.

"Try it."

"I can forbid you from coming onto our property," Ian shouted furiously. "You will be marooned here," he threatened, pointing a finger at the muddy beach.

"No we won't," said Dave. "We'll go home by your beach."

"We'll prosecute you for trespassing."

"A beach isn't trespassing."

"It is," screamed Ian.

"Anybody who needs to can use a beach," Dave told him smugly. "My father's a lawyer."

"Your father's a bum. He doesn't even have a job."

Dave charged. The boys rolled into the water. No one saw Yves Allard, the Loffts' houseman, sprinting down the lawn. Of course it was Bill who got caught.

*

Como House was a square villa of pink granite, surrounded by verandas. Nothing more remained of the seigneurial holdings of Vaudreuil, an estate that descended from the earliest days of New France. First one Marquis de Vaudreuil, and then another, had governed the colony. By the time their legacy had passed through a succession of spectacular wastrels and into the hands of Louis de Vaudreuil Lofft, it was a pretty threadbare relic. In the course of a scandalous career Louis ran through most of what was left. When he died the maiden heiresses of Vaudreuil got a big pink house and little else.

"Darling," Eleanor said, "I hear the ducks. It must be the children again."

"It's what the bloody ducks are *for*," muttered Nini from where she lay, disadvantageously arrayed for conversation, her naked body face down on a table. Bottles of rubbing alcohol stood on a shelf beside a stack of folded towels. A heat lamp painted Nini's skin bright pink. Her feet were enormous.

"I suppose it's Bill again," grunted Nini as they heard his earnest voice. "Perhaps if I crept out to the beach I could get Yves to capture *me*."

"It would not be seemly," said Eleanor.

"Exactly."

*

"Are you going to kill me?" asked Bill.

"Yes," said Yves.

"They will catch you," Bill pointed out.

"No," said Yves. "I will be careful."

"You might like to know that I am only six. That is a very young age for an English child."

"For a French too."

"I believe they still hang people for killing six-year-olds," Bill confided.

"Yes?"

"But not if you let them go," Bill assured him.

"Good," said Yves, "then I will only torture you."

*

Charlie dragged a length of electrical extension cord into his barn. He looped the cord over a beam and plugged it into a loose socket. A naked bulb now dribbled its light onto Noel, hunched on the dirty seat of an old Caterpillar, frowning at the instruments.

"I thought this was in working condition, Charlie."

"She's a fine machine, Noel," said Charlie.

"It won't start."

"Well, now," said Charlie vaguely.

"When you said this Cat was in working condition, I thought you meant now. I'd call that a reasonable inference."

"Yer a fine lawyer, Noel."

"Thank you."

"Your French Canadian, now. He has no understanding of the majesty of the law."

"And that proposition is connected to this machine, is it?"

"Them Allard boys," said Charlie, "they owned her last."

"Until you bought it from them."

"Our ancestors conquered the French Canadian," Charlie reminded Noel.

"Not exactly," Noel responded. "They conquered the French."

Charlie looked unhappily at Noel. "I could never work in the city," he muttered.

"I couldn't either."

"Talk circles around me."

"It doesn't work, then, this bulldozer?"

"Tell you what," allowed Charlie, "I'll fix her for nothin'. Then you do that gradin' job for me, also for nothin'. We'll call her even. No receipts, no cheques, no nothin'."

"No majesty of the law," said Noel.

*

"For Heaven's sake," thundered Nini, "do you want to turn his eyes to stone?"

"Sorry," said Yves. He put his hand over Bill's eyes and pulled him into the hall. The door slammed shut behind them. "Sorry," he said again, this time to Bill.

The hall was dark and smelled of wax. A pair of dejected wolfhounds sniffed sadly at Bill's hand, and padded back to their patch of sunlight near the stairs.

"It would be better outside," said Bill.

"I never tortured nobody," Yves told him glumly. "You are one kid."

"A kid," said Bill.

"Yes," agreed Yves, "one kid."

"Darling boy," boomed Nini, thumping barefoot into the hall. An orange kimono wrapped her tall body. "Dear, *dear* child," she roared, seizing Bill's hands and peering at his face. "So *just* like your delicious grandfather," she pronounced. "We cannot have you cowering in this fetid hole," she chanted, delivering a blistering smile at Yves. "Let's all go down to the veranda, shall we, and fill our bodies with *poisonous* sweets?"

"We were not going to throttle the ducks," said Bill, the beginnings of tears in his eyes.

"Dear boy," said Nini, "they are *there* to be throttled. An unthrottled duck is an insult to nature. Nothing so offends one's sense of fitness as some wretched little *duck* eating its way into middle age. That is why God put boys upon the earth, Bill." She took his hand and led him to the stairs. Yves trailed behind.

"Without boys, we would be overrun by ducks," Nini went on. "Kill them, I say, with bottle and with stone."

"I am only six," said Bill, a tear breaking loose and rolling down his cheek.

"I was clubbing them down like *flies* at your age,"

sang Nini, stepping onto the veranda.

"You are terrifying the boy," Eleanor observed.

"God," breathed Nini, oblivious, "how *smashing* to be young."

"Would you like some milk, Bill?" asked Eleanor.

"Or perhaps a glass of wine!" hooted Nini.

"I'll get you the milk," said Eleanor. "Don't be afraid of her."

"And wine!" roared Nini as Eleanor disappeared into the house. "What is in your little bag, Bill?"

"Books."

"How very *wise*."

"A dictionary is always helpful," said Bill, pulling out a muddy volume and holding it against his chest.

"I suppose you look up naughty words," Nini smiled.

"Dave is going to fuck Nick Jackson," said Bill, anxious to participate.

"Splendid," said Nini. "High time, too. David must be, what, ten?" She took a glass from Eleanor and thrust it to her nose.

"I seem to recall that he is twelve," said Bill.

"Is this the plum, darling?"

"It's the peach. The plum is not ready. I put it back."

Nini wrinkled her nose. "A bit *charming*, the peach, what? Bit on the *nice* side, yes?"

"The plum will be better," said Eleanor.

"I shall hope so."

"Margaret says my penis will fall off when I am ten."

"Rubbish, Bill. You will have a penis like a bull when you are ten."

"Margaret says she is an angel."

"They are *rabble*, Bill," piped Nini. "My ancestors would have driven the Currys from their sight with horsewhips." She examined the residue in her glass. "Put this out for the rats, shall we, darling?"

"Nothing will make me rush the plum," Eleanor stolidly maintained.

"Margaret is the female of the species," Bill announced.

"That may well be true," drawled Nini. "And when you are ten, like Dave, you must drag her off and have your manly way. But I must advise you that her kin are loutish to an advanced degree."

*

And later, leading him home by the hand, "Are you in school, Bill?"

"I don't want to go to school. I don't like nuns."

"Ha!" said Nini. "Small wonder. They are a martial band, Bill. Armed with a piece of chalk, a nun can pick the eye out of a robin at fifty paces. They can deliver chalk at a muzzle velocity that would shame a howitzer."

"I don't like them," said Bill.

"What a cornered nun can do with an axe handle, Bill, does not bear repeating to your shell-like ears."

"They're old."

*

"Do you know what a boner is?" asked Nick.

"Sure," said Dave.

"What, then?"

"You know." Dave swiped in the gloom at a tall cone of sawdust. Fed by trickles that leaked through from the saws above, these cones were always fresh and perfect.

They grew like stalagmites. Dave and Nick picked their way with ease through the forbidden maze.

"Of course *I* know," said Nick.

"Your penis fills up with blood."

"Yick!"

"You asked."

"I notice you don't have one."

"I don't need one."

"Dave," she said, facing him. "You should *always* have a boner when you're with a girl, especially if you love that girl."

"Yeah," said Dave.

"*Do* you love me?"

"Earth has not anything to show more fair," said Dave sullenly.

"That's great, Dave," said Nick, "but you can look that up in a book. It's not the same as a boner."

"Who said we have to fuck all the time?" demanded Dave. "Grownups don't fuck all the time."

"Grownups are not in love," said Nick. "Grownups are not the sweet bird of youth."

"Yeah," admitted Dave.

"Do you want to see my pussy?" She put a hand on his arm, steadying herself, slipping lightly from her jeans before he could protest. "You can touch it."

"It would be better if I washed my hands."

"I'm not asking you to operate, Dave."

"There could be germs."

Nick pulled her jeans back on in disgust. "Have you ever *seen* a pussy, Dave? I mean, are you *afraid* of it? Do you think I would *force* you into sex? We've known each other since we were kids."

"I hate it when you talk like that."

"I'm practically your *sis*ter."

"I would never touch my sister's pussy," said Dave with feeling. He grabbed a handful of sawdust and flung it at the floor. "You're always trying to push me around," he accused her. "Doesn't anybody ever listen to anybody around here?"

"Women have needs too, Dave. You don't have to get so mad."

"Everything's getting stupid."

"Don't you love me?"

"The male of the species knows when he should conquer the female. It's in his chromozones."

"What are chromozones?" asked Nick.

"They're in your loins."

"We better meet here tomorrow."

"You bet," said Dave.

"I really like your scarf. Ian Curry never wears a scarf."

"A gentleman is born to the purple."

"You better not be putting me on. I mean, about love."

"What light through yonder window breaks," said Dave.

*

"We were not going to throttle the ducks," Bill told Lucy.

"That's nice," said Lucy, noisily ransacking the fridge. "What happens to the food in this house, Bill?"

"We never buy any."

"Does it just evaporate?" asked Lucy, pushing a bottle of milk aside.

"No," said Bill. "Food doesn't evaporate. Water evaporates. Food rots. But first you have to buy it."

"Eh?" said Lucy, abandoning the fridge for a cupboard, staring in with a hopeless expression.

"Other mothers buy lots of food. That's how come they have it in their fridges. You have to buy a lot all at once."

"I guess that makes sense."

"It's called stocking the larder."

"I'm not a very good mother, Bill."

"You are an excellent mother. You are even a lawyer."

Lucy abandoned her search for food and came over to where Bill sat on a counter. She cupped his face in her hands and kissed him. "Where did I get you?"

"You bore me in your womb."

"Best idea I ever had."

"Are you mad at Dad?"

"Not really."

"Will we be in the poorhouse?"

"No, Bill."

"Good. I like it better here."

"Your dad is going to get some jobs with his bulldozer." Lucy turned away.

"Are you crying?"

"Yes." She sat on a bench below the tall, pointed windows that made the room a little like a chapel.

"I could help with the food. Miss Lofft said we could throttle her ducks."

"Maybe we could get the ducks to come over of their own free will," said Lucy. "We could promise them rooms of their own and use of the bathtub."

"That would be subterfooj," said Bill.

"Any kind of fooj is better than none, Bill."

"Is that a joke?"

"Yes."

"Pretty good," said Bill judiciously. "That's another

thing where you are better than other mothers. You're an excellent joker."

"Come on over here and sit on my lap, you dumb kid."

They stayed like that while Lucy cried, quietly. Bill asked if it was true that Noel was crazy. Lucy told him: people don't know what they're talking about, and you shouldn't pay attention to what they say about somebody as nice as your dad.

Bill agreed.

*

"A woman craves the spermatozoa of the male," Dave explained.

"Are you going to marry Nick?"

"Get real. I'm going to screw that broad until she can hardly walk." Dave examined his appearance in a mirror. He wore a shirt of Rufus's, a mighty volume of Egyptian cotton that swelled around him like a spinnaker. A paisley scarf hung sparely inside the gaping neck.

"Did you conquer her?"

"Her cherry is *finito*," Dave insisted. "Look at this." He pulled an illustrated medical text from his shelf. A pair of his grandfather's gold links, chased with the arms of Swan, dangled ineffectively from the wide, loose cuffs. Dave pushed these back to his elbows and opened the book at a section on female anatomy.

"Pussy city."

"It's all guts," said Bill.

"This is like X-ray vision. It looks better with skin on it."

"It would look better with clothes on it."

"These are the erectile tissues of the female genitalia," Dave indicated.

"It looks like there's something wrong." Bill frowned.

"Doctors make them lie like that so they can see their cunt."

"I would rather be a lawyer," said Bill.

"There is also erectile tissue in the areolae," Dave added. "That means their tits get hard when they're horny."

"I hate this book," said Bill.

"Bill," Dave warned, "if you don't learn to like girls and let your heart sing the strange sweet song of love you will turn into a hormone sexual. Hormone sexuals like men."

"I like men already."

"Get real, Bill. You don't like to *fuck* them."

"I don't like to fuck anybody."

*

Ode to a Caterpillar Tractor
by William de Saint-Victor Swan, Esq.

Lo! I do not think a father ought to drive:
A yellow Caterpillar when he goes to work:
A father should not e'en put on such dirty clothes:
And be a workman while other people smirk.

But anyway, a Cat is pretty nice:
And stronger than a bus or e'en trucks:
We could dig up a mighty pond:
And use it for a place to keep some ducks.

You could drive Caterpillars through a person's house:
And wreck it if that person laughed at Dad:
They would not like it if their house got broke:
But that would just be too darn bad.

*

"Bless me, Father, for I have sinned. What I want to know is, what if somebody *forces* you into a sin? Is that a sin? I mean, legally?"

"No one can force you to sin against God, my son."

"They can make it pretty hard to say no, Father. Especially if they're a girl."

"I think you must come to see me after I have finished here, my son."

"You bet," said Dave.

"Pray the rosary, and wait for me in the sacristy."

"No problem."

"Go in peace, my son."

"Old cocksucker," muttered Dave as he slammed out of the church.

*

"I'm not sure that tree is yours, Nini. It looks pretty close to Curry's line."

"Nonsense," boomed Nini.

"It might even be right on the line," said Noel.

"Don't be silly. Those trees have always been ours. Why would we have given one to a nameless creature like Gordon Curry? He sells things. He is a seller of *things*."

"Father would have known what to do," fretted

Eleanor, arriving with a tray of glasses.

"Father would have gotten into a drunken rage and ended by puking," Nini declared.

"He once sent Father some sort of cloth," said Eleanor, "in a box. For shirts. The cloth, I mean."

"Revolting stuff," hissed Nini. "*Striped*, for Christ's sake."

"Antoinette," enunciated Eleanor firmly, sliding her eyes to where Bill sat in a canvas chair, legs drawn up and chin supported on a knee, watching them as gravely as a bishop. Nini snorted.

"Father was a blackguard and a whoremonger, but thank God he never wore a striped shirt."

"He sent the cloth *back*," articulated Eleanor, attempting to wedge this word into Nini's path with enough force to make her notice Bill.

"He let his dogs piss on it first," corrected Nini, plucking a glass from Eleanor, "*then* he sent it back. Is this that peach again, darling?"

"This is the green currant."

Nini sniffed. "Bit *dressed up*, this, no?" She took a swallow and gazed at the sky. "Bit *aware* of itself?"

"I like it," said Eleanor stiffly. She handed Noel a glass. Nini smiled lavishly at her sister.

"I *quiver* for the plum."

"Pretty good," said Noel.

"The plum is not ready," Eleanor declared firmly. "When the plum is ready, then I shall decant the plum. Not before. Not later."

"Isn't she the Hun, though?" beamed Nini.

Noel's little Cat muttered through its pipes a dozen feet away. A thin breath of exhaust blew from its rusty stack. Behind it lay a slalom course of churned sod. Noel had failed in his attempt to follow a fading trail of wagon ruts along some trees.

"She's trickier than you'd think," he told them.

"I had no opinion about her one way or another," said Nini narrowly. They turned to study the old elm. Dead limbs poked from its spreading crown and patches of withered leaves showed where other branches were afflicted too.

"It's not quite dead, Nini. The Currys still use it." Iron furniture, painted white, stood in a large patch of shade on the adjoining lawn, shade which came from the disputed tree. Emblems of use littered the place. Cups from morning coffee. A newspaper. A striped parasol rose from the centre of a round table.

"They are a people obsessed with stripes," said Nini, her voice heavy with loathing.

"They have a cat," added Eleanor resignedly. No longer, her tone suggested, could the Currys be defended from her sister. They had a cat.

"It's only Curly," said Bill, but no one heard.

"Helen Curry is a harridan," trumpeted Nini. "She gathers in the shade of our tree and holds committees. We cannot bear it."

"I don't think I can pull it down anyway," said Noel. "It's too strong. You told me it was dead."

"Yves will saw it partway through," said Nini. "You pull it so it falls on our land."

"They could sue you."

"They wouldn't dare," said Nini serenely. "We bear an ancient name." She warmed to her theme. "It would scandalize the nation. The Currys would be torn apart by an outraged populace. I'll have a little slop of the dribble-berry, darling, if I may."

"Father was a senator," Eleanor reminded Noel. She dumped a measure of palish wine into her sister's glass.

"We are *icons*," bellowed Nini.

Yves's chainsaw was two-thirds through by the time Helen Curry exploded from her house and charged down the lawn.

"Stop!"

Of course it was too late. Noel finished the job, tugging the elm over with his little Cat. It landed with a terrific crash while Helen Curry ranted a dozen yards away.

Bill remembered to look up blackguard and whoremonger.

*

"When the girl's tits get hard," explained Dave, "it's time to ejaculate your semen into her."

"Sometimes a person doesn't have semen," fretted Bill.

Dave consulted the book that lay beside him on the bed. "Each millilitre of ejaculate has 100 million sperms."

"Unless you're little."

"It's nature's infinite wisdom," Dave assured him placidly.

"Daaa-aave!"

"Shit," whispered Dave, "that's Nick."

Bill looked out. "She's down there."

"Get away from the window," hissed Dave.

"You don't have to be mad at me. You're always mad at me."

"Don't whine."

"Well, I am not a whoremonger," Bill declared. He had spent two hours padding futilely about in the letter H on a hunt for this resplendent word, until a hunch had set him on its heels. Now he was determined to display its pelt while victory was fresh.

"You don't have enough sperms to be a whoremonger," Dave replied.

*

"It's that bean-bread, Mrs. Swan. I practised 'til I got it right. There are raisins in it too, because a man likes a sweet."

Lucy looked doubtfully at the reddish lump that sat on Nick's tray. "He's very picky, but I guess you know that."

"I like that in a man, don't you, Mrs. Swan?"

"It can be quite expensive."

"Money is no object," Nick declared, "not where it's for the love of a good man."

"I'll see if he's around."

*

"What's wrong with you, Dave?" asked Lucy when she found them. "You heard Nick."

"We were studying the book with girl parts in it," said Bill. "It's important for the male of the species to know the female and satisfy her yearning."

"That's nice, Bill," said Lucy. "Does the male of the species know that the female of the species is standing in the front hall waiting for him?"

"Sure," said Dave, getting up to follow Lucy.

"The male of the species might cheer up," she suggested. "He is not on his way to the scaffold."

"I brought you bean-bread," said Nick when Dave shuffled in.

"Great."

"It's got riboflavin in it, which is an essential vitamin. I looked it up."

"Sure."

"You were hiding from me," Nick accused him when they got outside. They headed for the mill.

"I was not hiding."

"Did you wash your hands?" she asked. "I'm not going to put up with your stalling."

"Sure," said Dave listlessly.

"I don't know. I just don't think you love me."

"Thou still unravish'd bride of quietness," said Dave.

"You just don't seem to *care*."

"Thou foster-child of silence and slow time."

"Oh shut up."

*

"Do I have to go to school?"

"You do, Bill." Lucy had the fridge open. "I think someone comes in here and steals our food."

"Nobody comes in," said Bill. "We just don't buy enough."

"What would I do without you, Bill?"

"You would still not buy enough," Bill told her, "even if I wasn't here."

Lucy opened a cupboard. "There's always pasta."

"We eat too much of that," said Bill. "It's an Italian food."

"What's wrong with that?"

"We are an English family, and proud of it."

Lucy shut the cupboard. "Is something bothering you, Bill?"

"Mostly school."

"I see." She sat beside him. "Tell me about it?"

"School might not be best for me."

"Why not, Bill? There will be a lot of kids there. New kids."

"I'm only six."

"That's the age they're looking for."

"At the Protestant school they are all English."

"We are Catholic."

"I think Protestant is better for English people to be. Then everybody can speak the same language."

"There are separate English classes. You *will* be speaking your own language."

"French kids don't like English kids."

"You don't know any French kids, Bill."

"Dave says the nuns are like Mongol horsemen."

"Maybe they'll let you feed their horses."

"The old ones are the worst," added Bill, unwilling to be jollied. "They can pick the eye out of a robin at fifty paces."

"And they do that, do they?"

"What a cornered nun can do with an axe-handle does not bear repeating."

*

"Surely this cannot be the peach?" Nini squinted at the glass.

"This is the pine cone."

"You are joking."

"It's experimental," Eleanor explained. Nini dropped

her nose to the glass, sniffed.

"A somewhat tar-like bouquet, I'm afraid."

Eleanor sighed. "You think I should pop it back into the cellar for a bit?"

"I think you should spray it on the weeds."

*

Lake of Two Mountains: a pair of bright hills above a river lake. Alston Vale and Hudson Heights, Hudson and Como: these were the English beads that necklaced the southern shore. All around lay the province of the French; downriver, splendid Montreal. To the north, beyond the near hills, the countryside rose into purple shapes and fled into wilderness at last, to those granite fastnesses where a paddle sinks at morning in a crimson lake and a small, lost plane can search in ever-widening circles, frantic, until its fuel is gone. No one will find it in that immensity. This is the country of Canada, shoaling northward after treasure, losing itself among wolves and broken mines until it returns at end of day to Alston Vale and Hudson Heights, Hudson and Como. Among such names a people paused, pegging their century to that brief shore and painting their houses white.

Heir to this, to every care that troubled man, Bill worried. A Roman citizen, he felt that cold wind out of Germany that blew into the streets of his palisaded town. Inside the pink stone library he ransacked books for answers. He learned of jade emperors who signed their names with a stroke of vermilion ink. He knew that the King of Burma was called the White Umbrella. He knew how to spell atrophy and solicitude, two excellent words. He went south with Charlemagne, riding in the vanguard, watching the forest through metal slits, and was relieved when the king led home his men to Aix.

Only he could not find how wings grew on girls.

*

"Sawdust is a kind of dirt. If you got sawdust stuck in your labium, it would be like dirt."

"Dave," said Nick, "I want to see your cock."

"Infection was discovered by Lister."

"I don't care if it was discovered by Columbus. You are going to touch my pussy. That's the way it works when a man and a woman fall totally in love. Love is a many-splendoured thing, Dave. You're not the only guy who knows poetry." She undid her belt and slipped out of her jeans. She kicked them onto a sawdust pile and stood in front of Dave in panties and shirt.

"I'm thinking of infection," he said dejectedly.

"From what?" demanded Nick. She took his hand and put it between her legs.

"It's soft," whispered Dave.

"*Touch* it."

He moved his fingers. "Gee."

"The opening is farther down."

"I like this part."

She spread her legs. "You're supposed to put your finger inside."

"Why?"

"For excitement," said Nick doubtfully.

"The whole finger?"

"Well," said Nick, sitting, leaning back, "do it slowly."

And he did. They were not quite sure they had it right: nothing exploded into showers of light; the smell of sawdust wrapped them as it always had, here in the underlight beneath the saws. They heard a screen door slam. They concentrated on each other's skin, how marvellous! Their eyes so clear and their skin so soft; their lips so strangely foreign and so brotherly.

*

Lucy's father, August Langwasser, was a tightly made and rather little gentleman who had separated himself from his beefy kinsmen in the village of Foresters Falls, descended the Ottawa River with his matriculation, installed himself in the capital, and shot forthwith into the mandarinate. He took a wife, fathered a daughter, acquired a house in Rockcliffe Park. By the time Gus Langwasser's wife succumbed to tuberculosis, her husband was so thoroughly dug into the affections of that crumbling knight who ruled the country as prime minister that the old man had walked behind the coffin, bareheaded in a cold wind. So had a huge and ferocious litigator from Montreal named Rufus Swan, who'd come up against the tiny figure of Gus Langwasser, found it to be made of granite, and befriended it. When Rufus came to the funeral he brought his son, a shy, shuffling mountain named Noel.

"I always felt that kid was looking for a ship to get on," said Gus now, down from Ottawa on a visit.

"That kid might have let us know a little earlier," snapped Lucy. "Then we wouldn't have mistaken him for a grown-up."

"Sorry," said Gus.

"Don't apologize, Dad. This is how I'm getting to be all the time. Mad, mad, *mad*." Lucy shook her head.

"Do you really want to get involved in this?"

"Come on, Luce. This is what parents do." A few bees patrolled the flowerbeds, butting sleepily about among the blossoms. Lucy stooped to snap off dead blooms. He watched her. "Your mother dug away at these things half her life. Never had any luck."

Lucy smiled. "Mother couldn't grow a dandelion." They stopped by a bright patch of marigolds. "So yellow," said Lucy.

"Is he all right? Noel?"

"How could he be all right, Dad?" She plucked a bloom and poked it carefully into her father's buttonhole. "I cry a lot."

"I'm not surprised," Gus frowned. "God these stink!"

Lucy nodded. "Sometimes I wish I'd planted *all* marigolds," she said, biting her lip. "Sometimes they last until the snow. You see them sticking out of the first snowfall." She straightened his lapel. "Do you miss Mom?"

"Not all the time, but more than I'd like."

"Daddy," she said, turning to hide her face, "I love him so much."

*

Gus loaded his grandchildren onto the train and took them upriver. "Maybe if I get the kids out of your hair," he'd said to Lucy. At Ottawa they changed to a steam-drawn local and puttered up into a broad valley of farms and loafing cattle, of shining fields and tin-roofed barns that glinted from ridges ten miles off. At Renfrew they left that line and climbed into the Madawaska Valley, making their way through a long, hot day into a country of sudden hills and abandoned lakes, of hamlets with churches and wooden stores, of pines and silver birch. From Barry's Bay they went by car, swooping over hills. They turned off onto a track that struggled through a stony pasture, wound into woods, and popped out at last in a little field high with yellow grass.

"There!" yelled Dave as the old car creaked through the grass toward a grove of thin red pines. They parked in the pines. Dave and Bill rushed down a short hill, past a shingled cabin, and threw themselves at a rope that dangled from a branch, screaming as they swung out over the lake.

Later they lay worn out with sun, sagging in ancient bunks, too exhausted to complain about mosquitoes. Loons called across the lake. They heard a soft wind soughing among pines, and wavelets breaking on a beach. Gus pushed another log into the woodstove and clanged the iron door.

"Grampa?"

"Right here."

"Is this where you grew up?"

"No, Bill. We lived in a town."

"This would be a good place to grow up."

"He's afraid of school," said Dave.

"I don't blame him."

"I thought you were smart, Grampa," said Dave.

"I hated school."

"I hate women worse than school," Dave yawned.

"He's always trying to conquer the female of the species," said Bill resentfully.

"Brave man."

For a week they rowed around the little lake, patrolling its sandy beaches or leaning overboard to search the lucid depths for a twitch of fin. They found an amazing trove of raspberries at a deserted farm. Gus tried to make a pie. The impromptu crust collapsed and he had to drag the whole mess smoking from the stove. "*Surprise aux framboises*," he pronounced doubtfully, and the boys fell upon it with spoons, giggling and howling "*surprise aux framboises*" through a spray of charred crust and crimson paste. They were sad to board the train. No one spoke as they wound out of those magic hills and onto the plain, changed at Ottawa, went down to Como.

*

Margaret had decided to fly. Her confidence in personal angelhood rested on a foundation as unshakeable as that which supported Bill's anxiety. Simply, Margaret knew that she would fly; Bill, that she would fall.

At the lake with Gus, Bill had made a careful study of birds. At home he had torn through shelves of books. Margaret surely lacked the requisites of flight. Lightness, he knew, was one of these.

"Their bones are hollow," he told Margaret.

"God makes angels," she responded, her face cupped full of sunlight and confusing innocence. "I can use my arms."

Bill trapped Charlie in his office. "Can God make a girl fly?"

"Well, now," said Charlie. "God, eh? Well, now. I'd have to think about that," and he fled. Bill brought the matter to Jesus Morris, wedging himself into the sawyer's booth alongside Jesus and laying out his tortured tale.

"Birds fly," said Jesus when Bill was through, and further than this he would not budge.

On flight day, Bill reported to Margaret's chosen launching pad, a stretch of shoreline where the bank rose sharply to a cedar hedge. The hedge would hide her from her parents' windows, in case their faith should prove less ferrous than her own.

Arriving early, Bill deposited a load of supplementary gear: an old umbrella and a discarded kite of Dave's. Margaret arrived and stepped to the bank. Bill produced a length of cord.

"We'll tie on the umbrella and the kite. Then you will get lift. A bird gets lift. That's how it flies."

"I am an angel," Margaret said. "Made by God," she added. And swiftly she unfolded her angel's arms, laid them out along the firmament, and toppled smartly forward into mud. It was a fall of only a yard but it winded Margaret. She gasped as she sprawled there on her belly by the lake.

"Hey," said Bill, scrambling down to the beach and kneeling by her head. His bare knees sank into sandy muck. He leaned over Margaret, his anguish clearly pictured in his face. Margaret began to cry.

"I'm not an angel!"

"Well, now," Bill said soberly. "I'd have to think about that."

"God didn't make me!"

"He made you a girl," Bill pointed out. Margaret sobbed more loudly. "Also," added Bill, "your father goes to work on the train." Margaret sucked in some mud, fell into a coughing fit, finally sat up. "Also," Bill offered, "you don't have to worry about a bulldozer."

"You are my boyfriend," Margaret announced.

*

Charged with a gulp of wine, Nini rolled from bed and began to storm about the house in a hail of vows.

"We must *unite*," she bellowed from the kitchen, raking through the cupboards one by one. "The Currys will fall upon Noel like pterodactyls. We must *organize*." Doors banged and the ground floor shook to her substantial tread. "Where *have* you hidden the Scotch?" she howled at Eleanor, who lay in bed with her snoring hounds nearby.

"Hmmm," breathed Eleanor.

"Plans must be formed," shouted Nini, charging upstairs. "Soon the tumbrels will be at our gate, and a cry of burghers." Nini thumped along the upper veranda and pushed open her door. "*Where* is the Scotch, darling?"

Later, like a pair of tweeden countesses, the Misses de Vaudreuil-Lofft issued from their gate on that pink Como morning, trailing a few thin scraps of plans and a pair of shuffling hounds.

"I am eager for the plum," Nini declared with firmness. "It is time, surely, for the plum."

"It is not quite time," insisted Eleanor.

"The raspberry was not a success."

"It would make perhaps a better cooking than a drinking wine," conceded Eleanor.

"It would make," said Nini, "a better wood-stain than a wine at all."

As they approached the Currys' drive, the nose of Helen's black sedan poked from her gate. Enraged by this affront, the wolfhounds rushed the car and boiled about its doors with drawn teeth. Helen blasted her horn. She rolled her window down an inch.

"They are in my way," she complained through the crack. A single long hat-feather bent against the glass. She twisted to glare at the dogs. A serge lapel brushed against the side of her face.

"You poor thing," said Nini, striding up and bending to shout through the crack. "You'll get that handsome orange lipstick all over your face."

"Those dogs should be on leads," cried Helen in a vain effort to seize the initiative. "They are a menace."

"They're *supposed* to be a menace," Nini said. "They're dogs."

*

"Do you think he's crazy?" asked Gus.

"I think he's got a kind of craziness, but I don't think he's crazy."

He held her hand as they walked. Lucy was pale but not delicate. She had an elfin quality that suggested some power beneath the skin, as if she could turn into bark, or vanish, or change you into stone. Her hair was drawn away from her face and held behind her neck in a clasp. She wore her clothes like accidents: they seemed to have nothing to do with her, but hid her true, green skin, her forest sheath.

"How about the boys?" asked Gus.

"They hardly seem to notice. I know they think about it a lot." They climbed onto the swing, sat. "They have tremendous loyalty," said Lucy. "I think they're afraid of being disloyal to Noel."

"Sure," said Gus.

"I'm worried about what will happen when school starts."

"The other kids?"

She nodded. "They can be pretty rough."

*

Among the fields and narrow, crooked lanes, the wolfhounds became more lively. They came upon a flock of mourning doves scratching in a sunny patch of gravel. The silent dogs sprang at them and a great squeaking of wings filled the air. They poked long noses under every weed and shot quick, anxious glances at each other with their bright brown eyes. A few of Charlie Hopkins's Jersey cows were somnolently grazing through the early hour. The hounds saw them and were over Charlie's fence in a bound, hurtling through a stretch of yard-high golden grass towards the astonished cows.

"Hector!" bawled Nini. "Ajax!"

Eleanor and Nini crossed the railway and penetrated that fatal grove of purple light, the maple wood. It was there they resolved to form a company. "Can't be that hard," Nini said. "Ought to be able to run one up in a day." Soon they were at the beaver pond. The hounds trotted out onto the dam and sniffed at some fresh mud and twigs.

"Poor Rufus," said Eleanor.

"But at least with a bang," sighed Nini.

"He would be pleased to know that we shall employ Noel."

"Nonsense," said Nini, "he would snort."

"Poor Rufus."

*

What am I doing? thought Noel. The attic sheltered him. He sat in warm darkness among boxes of his father's papers.

"This seems pretty real to me, Dad," he said out loud.

"Puzzling fellow," Rufus muttered into Noel's memory. Into the attic's dust came a smell of green saplings as Noel and Rufus pushed their way through to the pond. The day was cool and clear, remembered Noel. He recalled the softness of the air, heard again Rufus's voice.

"Would've thought that fellow would chew through those buggers in a few days," said Rufus, as if he were sitting in the eaves with his son, picking through their memories of those vanished days.

There'd been new construction on the dam and bright stumps glittering in the wood. The alligator had been sprawled at his favourite station on the dam, eyes closed, snout parked among twigs.

"Forlorn sort of fellow," Noel heard Rufus say, once again collapsing time, so that he seemed to sit there with Noel, two huge men in a little space beneath a roof, examining their past.

"He was trying to get warm," Noel confided now. Rufus nodded, as if he believed his son were right, and Noel added, "I like it here, Dad."

*

"Is Dad mad at us?" asked Dave.

Lucy faced her son. "No, Dave. Did you think so?"

"He spends a lot of time with Charlie."

"I guess he does."

"Ian says his father is going to sue Dad."

"He may."

"Ian is a shit-head."

"It doesn't surprise me, Dave."

"Yeah," said Dave. He put his hands in his pockets

and looked at the floor. "Ian said Dad was crazy."

"Well, as you said, Ian's a shit-head."

Dave made no noise at all. Simply, tears filled his eyes and rolled down his cheeks. "Is Dad crazy?"

Lucy pressed his head against her. "We're all a little crazy."

*

Except for a razor-thin annuity that dribbled in, a dollar at a time, Nini and Eleanor appeared to live on air. And yet a steady stream of goods and services supplied the mansion with its needs. Nini had never puzzled over this before. Now she did. Slumped into a wicker chair, she watched Yves throwing feed to the ducks. He had just finished mowing the lawn and a sweet smell of cut grass infused the air.

"Where do we get our money, darling?"

"Money?" said Eleanor. She had carried a small writing desk onto the veranda and was burrowing through a heap of papers. She lifted her head. "Nowhere. We are broke."

"I see," said Nini. "Then we shall be in trouble if Gordon sues us?"

"Not really," said Eleanor. "We have no money. There would be nothing to win."

"What about this house?"

"We don't own the house, dear," said Eleanor. "Father left the house in a trust."

"For whom?"

"Our heirs."

"We have no heirs."

"No," said Eleanor, bending back to her papers.

Nini regarded her with hostility. "Am I to be told nothing?" she demanded.

"You *hate* business," said Eleanor.

"But now we have decided to start a company, I am interested," Nini said patiently. "How do we pay Yves? How do we eat? How do we feed the wretched dogs?"

"Our financial affairs are not always scrupulous, dear."

"What, are we gangsters?" wondered Nini.

"We simply defer a lot of debts," Eleanor said apologetically.

"We *stiff* people," stated Nini, amazed. "How on earth shall we employ Noel?"

"We shall incorporate," said Eleanor, pushing a pile of papers aside and opening a ledger. "Father did it all the time."

"And pay Noel with what," asked Nini, "share certificates?"

"We shall borrow against the assets of the company," Eleanor said.

"And how do we get assets?" pursued Nini incredulously.

"We borrow them," said Eleanor without a blush.

*

"Do they give everybody a vaccination?" asked Bill from the fortress of his bed, looking for a little help on the ramparts, another good pair of eyes to help him scour that black plain for the restless machinations of adults. Dave flopped across Bill's feet, hung over the edge of the narrow bed to tinker with a broken wind-up toy.

"How come you keep these things?"

"Does it hurt?"

"Of course it hurts. It's a needle."

Bill's bedroom had no windows, only a door onto the second-floor veranda. Other doors connected his room to the main upstairs hall and a smaller back hall that led to a lonely bathroom and a crooked flight of kitchen stairs. This position between halls directed a certain traffic through Bill's room. It was something he liked.

"This way, everyone knows where I am," he had told Lucy when she'd offered him another room.

On one wall was a blackboard. Here the word "clitoris" had been carefully lettered and, in smaller letters, the explanation that this was "a homologue of the male penis, present in females of many of the higher Vertebrata." "Homologue" was also defined, and Bill would have been happy to explain "Vertebrata" as well, for he considered it to be an excellent word, and had omitted it only because of space. A bookcase held his supply of current reading. His other books—almost a hundred volumes—inhabited a trunk, where they were carefully arranged by category, or sometimes by size or colour. These classifications were often rethought by Bill, and a happy hour of unpacking and repacking would ensue.

"I already know how to read," said Bill.

"Forget it," said Dave. "You have to go."

Bill tugged the covers more tightly around his chin. "What about the French kids?"

"They're shits," said Dave. "They hate our guts."

"My guts are very small."

"But they're English guts."

"Will they hit me?"

"Don't worry so much."

"Okay," said Bill. He was quiet for a minute, watching his brother's silhouette.

"Is Mom going to get deborsed?"

"No, Bill," said Dave, "they can't get divorced. We're Catholics. What God hath joined together let no man put asunder."

"Oh," said Bill.

"That's the law of Holy Mother the Church."

"Oh." A whippoorwill began its liquid call nearby. They listened until the bird moved off and resumed its call, farther away but still loud.

"I think we should be Protestant," said Bill.

"We can't," said Dave. "The sacrament of confirmation makes us soldiers of Jesus Christ."

"Protestants have Jesus Christ."

"Forget it, Bill."

*

And so the higher Vertebrata prepared for school. Lucy brought out the boys' new clothes. This part Bill enjoyed. He smelled the boxes they came in, took out the sheets of tissue paper, folded and stored them in his trunk. Lucy handed him an Indian belt with a beaded design. Bill gasped with pleasure, thrust the belt into his new jeans, and rushed off to the sawmill to consult Jesus Morris about the secret meaning of the belt's design. Dave pulled on a snap-brim cap.

"Mom, this is *neat*," he told her with a shining face.

"It's the Great Spirit," said Bill, hurrying into the kitchen when he returned. "Jesus says this green part here, it's the Great Spirit."

"They say everything is the Great Spirit," said Dave.

"It *is*," insisted Bill.

"Come on, Dave," said Lucy. Dave shrugged, set his

cap at an angle, and sauntered off to find a mirror. Bill opened his lunch box, took everything out. He unwrapped his sandwiches and peeled back the bread, scrutinizing the contents as if he were a jeweller with a possibly defective gem. Finally he sighed, put everything back in different order, closed the tin lid with a snap. He put the box aside and emptied his knapsack for the third time, meticulously ranging its contents on the table. Bud Jackson had presented him with a set of pencils, his name stamped on each one.

"These are a prize possession," he confided to Lucy, replacing them in his pencil box and sliding the long lid shut. Finally Lucy watched them go, trudging up the path to wait for the taxi. Bill's mood slid downward fast. Elevated at first by the pencils and the smart new belt, it soon returned to gloomier subjects.

"A nun can kill a bird at fifty paces."

"Hmmm," said Dave, toying with his hat.

August's heat had overflowed into September. Soon they were sweating. A heavy, sweetish smell of rubber lay along the road in that still morning air. Dave took off his cap, fiddled with the snap, put it on.

"Superior neat," he pronounced.

"Will you take me to the partridge nest?" asked Bill.

"They're all gone. There'd only be the nest."

"Will you?"

"Sure," said Dave, "next time we hike."

At half past eight the taxi beetled round a curve and squeaked to a stop. The door opened and Dave climbed in. Bill stared. Finally an arm reached out and yanked him in. From a tumble of legs and shiny blue serge skirts, Bill looked up at the hairiest lip he had ever seen on a girl.

"Who's he?" laughed Lise Allard. *Oo-zee?*

"William de Saint-Victor Swan," said Bill, clutching

his lunch box to his chest.

"My brother Bill," said Dave.

"Beel?" said Lise. "Beel, Beel, *centre ville*," she chanted, blowing the smell of an alien breakfast into Bill's face. She hauled him up and placed him on her lap. Bill tried to clamber off but she tightened her arms and held him there. She began to rock him. "Beel, Beel, *centre ville*," she crooned her meaningless rhyme.

"I'd like to get up, Dave," said Bill.

"Yeah," said Dave. "Forget it."

"*Tu es très joli*, Beel," Lise breathed into his face. Bill pulled away. Lise dealt him a blow with a hand like a board. His ears rang and he felt his skin burn.

"Dave?"

"Leave him alone, Lise," Dave said without much hope. Lise ignored him.

"*Reste tranquille*, Beel," she laughed. "Beel, Beel, *reste tranquille*." She laughed again. "*Je t'aime*, Beel. *Tu es très joli, très très joli*."

"She likes you," said Dave.

"She smells like eggs," Bill said. "I hate her guts."

"Guts?" Lise breathed into Bill's face. "Who's guts?"

"My guts," said Bill.

"*Reste tranquille*," Lise told him. "Stay quiet."

"Okay," said Bill.

*

While Bill rode off to school, separated by but a few thin thicknesses of cloth from the sturdiest homologue of the male penis that ever ground its teeth, his parents remained behind to drift about their empty house. Noel had not much work yet for his Cat. It was not clear he even wanted work. Lucy moved through the halls, confused and angry, feeling Bill's absence keenly, sometimes talking to herself, sometimes out loud. When all at once they were beguiled by the day, plucked right into it, a fine bright day with a whole parade of flawless clouds that bowled downriver on their way to Montreal. It pulled them onto the veranda, where they met at noon as if they'd planned it, which they certainly had not.

"Let's go over to Dad's," said Noel, with a big sheepish look.

"Why?"

"Let's just go," he said again, shyly.

Noel shoved a bottle of gin into a knapsack, grabbed a bag of ice, some bread and cheese. Lucy came back downstairs, slim and lovely in a cotton dress, and off they went. They ended up a few hours later, flushed and pretty drunk, tumbled into bed in a big spare room that overlooked the lake, those clouds. But Noel and Lucy's marriage was not a structure to be righted by one hot grapple and an afternoon of gin. Its list was too pronounced. God bless them both, they went home sad, finished that day sadder than they had begun.

*

The parish school of St-Thomas-d'Aquin occupied a narrow, brown-shingled building on a residential street in Hudson. A single maple rose in front, its grey trunk hatched with ciphers carved by years of knives. In its branches lived a population of squirrels, a band of fat black shapes that charged about among the children, foraging for scraps. Sometimes one would come too close to a group of predatory older boys, and its thick tail would end the day on a handlebar. Otherwise they were left alone and envied, emblems of freedom whose sudden rushes across the roof reminded the prisoners inside of wider skies.

As the taxi pulled away a bell began to ring. Dave led Bill inside and took him down a hall that smelled of chalk. At the end waited a tiny nun. A few silver hairs escaped from beneath her coif and floated beside her head. A silver crucifix shone against the white starched bib that covered her from chin to waist.

"What, can this be William?" she called. Her voice was surprisingly musical.

"She knows who I am," said Bill, holding tightly to his brother's hand.

"They have a list," explained Dave.

"Well?" said the nun. She was no taller than Dave, but managed to regard Bill down the length of her nose as if from a great height. "You say, 'How do you do, Sister Agatha,'" she prompted. Bill stared.

"Say it," Dave ordered.

"How do you do, Sister Agatha," said Bill woodenly.

"I am very well, thank you, William, and how are you?"

Bill stared.

"Say, 'Fine,'" hissed Dave.

"Fine," said Bill.

"You say, 'I am fine, thank you, Sister Agatha.'"

"I am fine, thank you, Sister Agatha."

"You may go and take your seat. It is in the third row. You share a bench with that little girl." Sister Agatha pointed. "Go." Bill walked uncertainly into the room. "He looks like a nice little boy," Sister Agatha said to Dave.

"He's pretty young."

"I shall try to remember that," said Sister Agatha

firmly, and she handed Dave a card. On one side, printed in heavy capitals, a short prayer; on the other, a picture of Our Lady of Perpetual Help. "Pray to Our Lady, David," she told him, before she followed Bill inside and shut the door.

*

"Let's make it a smashing big company, shall we?" said Nini.

"I thought you found this dreary."

"We'll make money by the cartload."

"It is not so simple," replied Eleanor, offended at Nini's sudden intrusion into the world of the bottom line, where previously Eleanor had ruled alone.

"The Glorious Goliath Excavating and Levelling Company," trumpeted Nini. "The contracts will come *pouring* in."

"It is not a dignified name."

"We shall drive to the bank with *sacks* of lucre."

"We have no car."

"We shall have a car," said Nini sternly. "Let there be an end to this prudence. We are not Protestants."

"Whatever Father may have done, Nini," said Eleanor severely, "he always used a dignified name."

"And only the best letterhead."

"I don't know," said Eleanor.

"Engraved," commanded Nini.

"We shall need credit."

"Demand it."

"A good stout bond," said Eleanor, "with visible watermark. Perhaps a buff colour?"

"See to it," said Nini.

*

Sister Agatha took her place in front, at a small desk on a dais. A picture of Our Lady of Perpetual Help gazed blankly out at the faces of the first and second grade. A steady thumping of pacing nun came through the ceiling from a class above. A raised voice sounded from the hall, a torrent of French words that ended in a slap. Someone whimpered. Another burst of angry words, then silence.

"Now we shall introduce ourselves," said Sister Agatha, unperturbed by whatever violence might stalk the corridor outside her class. "Turn to the person sharing your bench. Say 'How do you do,' then say your name."

"How do you do. Sally," said Bill's deskmate.

"It says 'Sarah'," said Bill.

"What?"

"The card there, on your desk. It says your name is Sarah."

"My name is Sally."

"It says 'Sarah'."

"You think you're so smart."

"No."

She leaned close to Bill. "Piss."

"Hey," said Bill loudly.

"What's the matter, William?" asked Sister Agatha.

"She called me piss," said Bill. Sally started to cry.

*

"How'd it go?" asked Dave when they got home.

"Sister Agatha hit me."

"How come?"

"Because Sally called me piss."

"Yeah," said Dave, "any bad word, they hit the boy. Did she give you a picture after she hit you?"

Bill took out a card of Our Lady of Perpetual Help. "When Mary had the baby Jesus, he was not born of the sin of lust."

"She got into that already?"

"When God picked Mary to be his mother, he didn't want her to have to sleep with her husband. So she didn't."

"Bill, I've been there, okay?"

"God said, 'My thoughts are not as your thoughts, nor my ways as your ways.' "

"Aw, shit."

"God didn't need a mother to get born," said Bill. "He just decided to have one. He was just doing a favour. He could have been born without a mother, because he is the most high. But when he decided to use a mother, so he could be born the normal way, he wanted his mother to be free of the sin of the flesh."

"I hate it when you're like that. Don't you forget anything?"

"It's the word of God."

"It's the nuns."

"They are married to God."

"Jesus, Bill, she really gave you the whole shot."

"There are certain truths, and they are sublime."

"How about the truth that nuns have a pussy too? Did she get around to that?"

"They are holy vessels."

"There's a secret tunnel that goes from where the priests live to the convent. Late at night the priests sneak through, even though it's full of spiders, and have an assignation with the nuns. Love is a many-splendoured thing. Even for nuns."

"It would be a sin."

"Priests can do whatever they like. It's part of their job, okay? Then they give themselves confession and they're clean."

"It would be a sin."

"So what? Even jacking off is a sin. Touching a girl's tits is a sin. It's a sin to put your tongue in a girl's mouth. That's why they have confession."

"I don't want to put my tongue in a girl's mouth."

"You don't even want to fuck one."

"No."

"They give you your first confession this year anyway, so when you're old enough to get a boner, you'll be ready."

"Nick doesn't have confession because she's a Protestant."

"She is still the female of the species. That broad is dying for coition."

Later, Bill became inexplicably sad. Retreating to his room, he sat on his bed with his fists squeezed tight and cried as quietly as he could. Dave came in and found him. He sat beside Bill and stared out through the veranda, through trees to the lake.

"Come on," Dave said finally, "we'll go for a hike."

"To the partridge nest," said Bill, following him downstairs.

"It's too far," said Dave. "We'll go to the turtle pond."

*

Nick spied them as they left their gate, caught up to them behind Charlie's house. Charlie's farm lane straggled out of his yard, soon became a slot between two fields. They marched along this dusty way until they reached a pasture where Charlie sometimes kept his little Jersey bull. Disappointed that this dwindling menace was not there, they climbed a fence and crossed the pasture to their goal.

Each spring, freshly charged with melted snow, this pond began its long haul into summer, dragging with it a number of luckless fish, a surly mob of redwings, frogs the size of rabbits. The green air swarmed with iridescent pins as dragonflies went darting after prey. By late summer the redwings had mostly left. What frogs and fish remained were stunned with lethargy. The pond itself had shrunk to half its size. One creature thrived in this: the turtle. As their world collapsed into a slimy sink, the turtles paddled stoutly on, poking their ancient, shrivelled heads through algae blooms and spreading their patient brand of death.

At one end of a raft of slab and muddy logs sat Bill, beside an arsenal of rocks. Dave and Nick poled away from shore, pushing through a channel that pierced a wall of bulrushes, gaining the open pond. Weeds and algae collected against the advancing raft. Bill reached for a yellow lily as they glided by, dipping his hand beneath the surface to clutch its stem.

"Don't do that, Bill!" warned Dave. "This place is full of snappers!"

Most turtles in Charlie's pond were harmless, a smallish, bright green race with exaggerated domes that were speckled with white dots. These were easily caught. Then their legs would flail away, claws scratching against the fingers that held them by the shell. Often their captors would carry them away, releasing them at a distance and waiting while they cranked their old-men's heads around, decided which way lay home, and plodded off. They always knew the way.

But no one touched the snappers. Not with hands.

These lay in mud, in sullen readiness, or heaved their blackish, rough-spined shells onto rocks. The children sought them out in avid dread. This time they found one on a tip of log against a bank.

"We'll coast in," whispered Dave. Nick crept forward to man the rocks. Dave pushed carefully. Nick stretched out her arm and grasped a rock. All summer lay in that slow, murderous tableau: the tightened arm, the turtle's sun-besotted sleep, that purposeful approach. Suddenly the turtle's head clicked round; Nick threw. In a splash of rock and plunging shell their quarry vanished.

"You got him," said Dave as they poled back, "for sure."

"I wish we went to the same school," said Nick.

"Yeah."

"Do you miss me, Dave?"

"I feel a nameless sadness o'er me roll."

"I like your cap."

"Irish tweed."

"You are a gentleman."

"Yes," agreed Dave. "You have to be born to it."

*

Autumn came whisking down the river soon enough, through crystal dawns and stiff blue afternoons. The turtles burrowed into mud and a skin of ice grew out from shore. Bill and Dave opened their mouths and blew out puffs of breath, watching them cloud in the cold air. Their mouths stayed open in delight. The maples went yellow and red. Dead leaves with crusts of ice broke underfoot. Autumn tightened on the land until it snapped. From the sawmill came a whine of saws. A launch's horn blew from the lake, announcing that one of the Allards would soon appear from the mist towing a boom of logs.

"I hate Lise Allard."

"She is a slut," said Dave absently.

"She is a rotten cunt."

"Bill," said Dave, surprised, "if anybody hears you say those words, you're going to be in big trouble, okay?"

"Okay," said Bill.

"Especially that slut Sally," cautioned Dave. "That broad is poison to you."

"Sister Agatha wouldn't like it either," ventured Bill.

"No kidding."

"Girls are a lot of trouble to the male of the species," said Bill.

"They are full of hormones that make them crazed with lust," said Dave.

"They stink like wormshit," offered Bill, anxious to click what castanet he could.

"It's their hormones that give them their tits and cunt, and make sure they don't have beards when they grow up."

"Lise has a moustache," Bill pointed out.

"Yeah," Dave agreed. "There's something wrong with that broad's hormones."

"She has tits, though."

"You bet."

"But I don't think anybody would want to put his sperms into her stomach."

"The sperms go into the uterine cavity," said Dave.

"It's a good thing God didn't pick Lise to be the Blessed Virgin," said Bill, ranging into other pastures. "I wouldn't want her to be Jesus's mother."

"Bill," asked Dave, "what planet are you from?"

"The third planet from the sun."

Into this moment of golden discourse squeaked the

taxi. It rocked to a halt beside them. The door opened.

"Beel," cried Lise.

*

"Margaret! You startled me." Lucy had no idea how long Margaret had been standing there in the kitchen, behind her. The child smiled her rather witless smile. Over one arm slumped the boneless shape of Curly, the tips of his ears smartly picked out in glossy pink. With Margaret's free hand she held a bag.

"This is for Bill," she told Lucy. Lucy took the bag and looked inside. There were two packages wrapped in bright paper and clumsily tied with ribbon. A strong smell came from one of the packages, and damp patches had appeared through the paper.

"I guess I should leave these for Bill to open, should I?" asked Lucy.

"They are for Bill," repeated Margaret.

Lucy wrinkled her nose. "Should I be putting these in the fridge, Margaret?"

"They are food," said Margaret. "Bill is my boyfriend, and he never gets enough to eat."

"Did your mother give you these? Is one of them meat?"

"It's for Bill. One is a meat course and the other is a dessert course. He is a male."

"He's explained that to you, has he?"

"He is my boyfriend."

Lucy shoved the bag into the fridge. "You and Nick must have the same adviser."

*

Nini and Yves sailed out of Como on a day so crisp you could have cut it into pieces with a pair of shears. The old truck pitched through a landscape of lacy trees, of mansions, of children shepherded by woolly dogs. They drove through Hudson, Hudson Heights, and Alston Vale. At the end of this tossing road a flood plain widened into farms, and they came to Rigaud.

Here were the battered streets of a country town, its sagging balconies and rusting roofs. A loafing commerce dawdled in and dawdled out again. Entrusted with this idling freight of souls was the Catholic church, a pompous heap of stone and bells teeming with clergy. It raised itself from the muddy banks of the Rigaud River with all the self-possession of the Sainte-Chapelle. There the priesthood of Quebec trooped blithely through a century that elsewhere had passed on. With Vatican complacency they governed their sturdy flock, and whatsoever was loosed in Rigaud was also loosed in heaven.

On the secular side was a less formally entrenched but more efficient apparatus: the single, vast, presiding form of Léopold-Anatole Gingras.

Léopold-Anatole possessed power in a way that Talleyrand would have understood: he had it because it belonged to him. When people thought of something needing to be done, they thought of Léopold-Anatole. And they were right. So many strings fetched up in the hands of this country advocate, it was said, that if he sneezed, half the noses of Quebec would twitch in sympathy.

Léopold-Anatole was not powerful from greed, or not exclusively. His imagination was too restless. He was a tinkerer. Like Rufus Swan, he could not see a thing amiss without giving it a prod. He looked like a minister of the *ancien régime*, fat and gallant, autocratic, incapable of surprise. Nini sat now in his office watching him reconnoitre an appalling heap of files.

"Ah." He tugged one out. "The Glorious Goliath Excavating and Levelling Company, Limited," he intoned. "An august name, no?"

"I don't suppose you'd have a splash of wine around here, would you, darling?" Nini wondered.

"August," repeated Léopold-Anatole, as if she had not spoken. "Its prospects, mademoiselle, are also august?"

"Its prospects are entirely conjectural, Maître Gingras," admitted Nini, "as I suspect you know."

"I understand," sighed Léopold-Anatole. "Life is often conjectural. A fine word, conjectural."

"But will they like it at the bank?"

"Alas," he murmured, "not." He proffered a surprisingly neat folder. "Your company charter, mademoiselle."

"Eleanor says you are to keep it," said Nini. "Put it with the rest of our lives."

"You honour me," he replied, struggling to his feet. "Your father was my mentor, which you know, and a great champion of the region." Léopold-Anatole smiled distantly. "It is the right word, champion?"

"It is the wrong word. Scoundrel is the right word."

Léopold-Anatole accepted this correction with equanimity, sighing deeply and spreading his hands in a gesture of resignation that seemed to reduce whatever perfidy there might have been to the comfortable dimensions of rural vice. "We loved him," he said simply.

"You loved not wisely," said Nini. They emerged into the street, where Yves waited in the spavined truck. "Glorious Goliath's fleet," proclaimed Nini, "and its first employee. We understand," she added, mistress of finance, "that there are tax advantages attached to employing Yves corporately."

"Indeed," observed Léopold-Anatole, "that is true. The advantages are, of course, only of interest if there is income." Nini gave the old man a hard stare. "Your servant, mademoiselle." He raised her hand to his lips.

They stopped once on the way home, when Nini sent Yves for a pint of Scotch. By the time the pickup finally turned in at Como House, headquarters of the Glorious Goliath Excavating and Levelling Company, Limited, the vice-president of that somewhat notional enterprise was sound asleep.

*

"Are you up there, Noel?" Lucy stood by the ladder.

"Sorry?" Noel's head appeared in the opening.

"Are you coming down?"

"I'm looking for those drawings you did when we went to Venice."

"Throw them out," said Lucy. She sat on the bottom rung and put her elbows on her knees. "We were so young."

"That time we drank wine for breakfast," said Noel from the dark opening, "remember that?"

"I got sick."

"Not really, but you were pretty drunk."

"You hired that fancy motorboat and we went to the Lido."

"The water was filthy."

"We swam anyway."

"I took a room at that big hotel so we could make love without going all the way back."

"They didn't want to rent it to us."

"Oh yes, they were happy to rent it. They just wanted to charge more."

Grinning down through the trapdoor, Noel looked boyish, more graceful, less huge than he really was.

"Why don't you come on down," whispered Lucy.

"I think I know where those drawings are," said Noel, looking back into the attic.

"Noel?"

"I'll just be a minute," he said, withdrawing into the attic again. Lucy heard the ceiling creak as he crept across the beams, into the past.

*

"Lise wants me to marry her."

"Is that what she said, Bill?" Lucy was exploring the fridge.

"She said I would be her husband."

"Has Dave been throwing food out again?"

"Just wieners."

"Hot dogs?" said Lucy. "*Hot* dogs?"

"He said they were poison. They're made with the guts of animals. They use whatever guts they can't sell like ordinary meat."

"*As* ordinary meat," corrected Lucy.

"They grind the guts up and squeeze them into a tube, and sometimes there's even cow poop and ground-up eyes and cow feet and nostrils and ear-drums."

"I understand the principle, Bill."

"Who wants to eat ground-up poop and eyes?"

"I'll murder that kid," muttered Lucy. She pulled out a package and smelled it. "I think this has gone bad."

"We never buy enough food," said Bill, "and when we do buy it, it goes bad."

"It's an area of life where your mom has always been rotten, Bill."

"Maybe you should be a lawyer."

Lucy shut the fridge and looked at Bill. "Let's have a cookie."

"I think Dave threw them out."

"I hid some."

"I would like Lise to leave me alone," said Bill as he picked the chocolate chips out of a cookie and ate them one by one. "I don't want to get married."

"I don't blame you."

A saw whined into a log, a lazy sound, indolent, its quality of labour stripped away by the placid day, by a view of sparkling water, by high, toppling clouds. A rise in temperature had filled the air with a smell of grass, of pine gum oozing onto bark, of damp earth. Into these milling smells came a great balloon of scent, of fresh air soaked in sawdust and rolled uphill from the lake.

"I don't think I would like to put my penis inside Lise's uterine cavity."

Lucy nodded. "It doesn't sound very attractive."

"She has a moustache and smells like sweat," said Bill.

"I'm sorry to hear it."

With a falling sound the saw shut down. A rumbling of chains echoed from the slides. Through a thin screen of brittle leaves they watched Archie and Jesus wander to the shore. Archie stood ankle-deep in sawdust, holding a boat by its short bow chain. Jesus climbed in; they pulled away for Oka. Oars rose and fell, grabbing at the silver surface of the lake as if it were a cloth, dragging it aside in wrinkled heaps to show black water underneath. Behind them as they pulled away they left these pairs of wrinkles on the lake, each pair slowly smoothing out, closing again, mending itself upon that sliding black until the silver cloth was once more whole.

"Where are we going to get the money to maintain our way of life, Mom?"

"Where do you get these phrases, Bill? What is our 'way of life'?"

"It's how we live. How you live, that's what class you're in. We're in the upper class, but we are electric."

"Eccentric."

"Compared to other families we are crazy. Other fathers never quit their jobs. They keep their jobs and they go to work on the train."

"Does that sound like the best way to live?"

"For a father."

"Don't you like your dad the way he is?"

Bill frowned. "I worry about him."

"You worry a lot, Bill."

"Somebody has to."

"Oh," said Lucy. "I forgot. Margaret's left you a present."

"I hope she didn't leave Curly."

"It's food."

"She tried to give me Curly for an engagement present."

"You're engaged?"

"She is not Catholic."

"Let's see what you got."

Bill took the paper bag from the fridge and put it on a counter. He examined it suspiciously. Finally he reached in and drew out a package, the smaller one. It was bright green, with a green ribbon.

"It's soft," he frowned, as if this quality was to be held

against it. Lucy handed him a pair of scissors. He snipped the ribbon and peeled away the paper. A mess of chocolate cake came apart with the paper, clinging to the wrapping in lumps.

"I guess that's the dessert course," said Lucy.

"Better not show it to Dave," said Bill. He retrieved the second package. Larger and heavier and apparently moist, it had almost rotted through its handsome gold wrapping. Bill snipped the ribbon. Inside was a piece of steak. "Meat," said Bill.

"I bet Helen Curry doesn't know about this," said Lucy.

"Probably Curly licked it," Bill worried. "We'd better throw it out."

"Not bloody likely," Lucy murmured.

*

Clementine Jackson and her painting party sat at their easels, daubing dutifully away while autumn somersaulted past behind their backs. Helen Curry sat among them, a huge form perched dangerously on a folding stool. She was not a regular member of Clementine's group, but wanted to be. Helen's ambitions were as vast as her exertions, and Clementine Jackson's rung was one upon which she longed to plant her mighty shoe. Clementine knew this.

"You want to breathe some cobalt into that sky, Helen," she observed. "It is too pretty."

"I would think cobalt too sombre," Helen bristled.

"Just lash a little of it in there, dear," Clementine told her serenely. "You'll see I'm right."

"But," persisted Helen, "I paint what I see."

"Then you must abandon hope, my dear."

*

"Your mom is pretty rough," said Dave.

They were in the alley between Charlie's office and the forge.

"Yeah," said Nick.

"She might see us."

"No."

"Your mom could see through bricks."

"My mother didn't see us, Dave. So drop it." She led him into the mill yard, marching straight around to the sawdust pile. They floundered through loose sawdust and slid in by a narrow opening. They were under the mill. Light slatted through rough planks and fell onto the oily, earthen floor. Dave rubbed sawdust out of his hair.

"My pockets are full of this shit."

"You shouldn't swear in front of your girlfriend," said Nick.

"You don't have to be so bossy."

"We have plighted our troth," Nick declared in an injured voice, "but all you seem to do is worry about my mother."

"This is my best shirt," grumbled Dave.

"Yeah. The cuff links are nice."

"We are an ancient line," Dave affirmed, poking sawdust out of huge, folded cuffs.

"When a man takes care with his appearance it shows he cherishes his beloved." She led him into their hideaway. She faced him. "We'll take *all* our clothes off."

"Sure," he whispered.

"No one can hear us, Dave." She slipped out of her jeans. "We're secret here."

"Yeah," whispered Dave.

They clung together awkwardly. She groped between his legs and they fell clumsily into the sawdust. She kissed him fiercely on the lips, squeezing his face between her hands and staring with open eyes. After a clumsy moment, Dave returned the kiss.

"Boy, are you ever horny," Nick told him. "You've got a boner."

"Yes," whispered Dave, proud.

"We won't be able to do this when it's cold."

"No," he breathed.

"We'll have to fuck at my place," Nick stated, seizing some decisive edge, a position of leadership, as naturally hers. By his silence Dave acquiesced, too bowled over anyway by a sense of largeness, of grandeur almost, to more than mumble.

*

A heavy rain drummed on the tin roof and rattled in the drains. Every room of that ramshackle mansion filled with metal sounds of rain, with a cold, autumnal sense of frigidness waiting an inch away.

"It's cold against the walls," said Bill. "I don't think we have enough heat in our house." Dave grunted from his book. "We never have enough heat," persisted Bill. "I think a father is supposed to make sure a furnace will do proper heating. If the furnace doesn't do proper heating, then the father is supposed to fix it." Dave turned a page. "If the father can't fix it," Bill went on, "then he should get a workman to come and fix it."

"Shut up, Bill."

"I hate it when you tell me to shut up."

Dave retied the cord that held an Edwardian smoking

jacket close to his thin body. "I could lend you one of my scarves," he offered Bill. He proceeded to a mirror, checked his own lavish scarf. "Silk is good for a chilly night. You knot it loosely, with a devil-may-care nonchalance."

"Never any food," muttered Bill, "never any heat. This family is not prepared for every eventuality."

"You don't even know what 'eventuality' means," muttered Dave.

"It means what could happen," said Bill. He huddled in a windowseat. The sleeves of one of Lucy's sweaters flopped around him. Rain pounded the windowpanes. Bill's knees were drawn up. He looked cold and ready to cry.

"Come here," said Dave, retrieving his place in the world of physiology, flipping a few pages, finding what he wanted. Bill joined him on the bed. Dave pointed to a fetus curled in the womb.

"That's how they start. The spermatozoa of the male implants the baby in the mother's stomach."

"It's got a big head," said Bill.

"The head shrinks later. At the same time as the baby grows in the stomach, the girl's tits fill up with milk."

"I thought you said the baby was in a mother."

"First they are girls. Then mothers."

"If mothers have milk in their tits, how come we have to buy it?"

"There's never enough."

"There's never enough of anything," said Bill.

"In order for God to get more souls and make the Church Militant into an instrument of the Holy Ghost, he lets people join in holy union. Then you can legally fuck."

"God is the Supreme Bean."

"That's got nothing to do with it, Bill. You probably haven't gotten any further than the difference between original sin and venial sin and mortal sin."

"If you have mortal sin and you die," said Bill, "you go straight to hell where you dwell in the tormenting fire for all eternity. They never let you out."

"That's what I mean," said Dave, "you're still on the sin part. You haven't even had your First Communion. Until then they don't tell you about the other sacraments, like Holy Matrimony. You have to be older."

They heard footsteps, and the familiar creak of someone ascending the front stairs. Lucy appeared in the doorway.

"Bedtime, Bill."

"It would be better if I stayed with Dave," Bill said earnestly. "I think the furnace is broken."

Dave shook his head. "You're the only person I know who's afraid of rain."

"Can I have a holy candle?"

"You can light one candle on your altar," Lucy told him. "I'll come up later and kiss you good-night."

They padded into Bill's room and stopped at his altar, an old table draped in a grey flannelette blanket and shoved against a wall. Its tabernacle was a cardboard box shrouded in a towel. On top of the tabernacle was a plaster Mary standing on a terrestrial globe. Beneath her bare feet, its fanged mouth gaping in agony, writhed the crushed serpent.

"That snake gives me the creeps," said Dave.

"It's the devil."

"I know who it is. It looks like it could bite her in the foot."

"The devil could not hurt God's mother." Bill had filled two vases with bulrushes. These rose, strangely pagan, at either end of the table. A book of matches and a small collection of votive candles occupied the tabernacle.

"Do you *pay* for this stuff?" asked Dave.

"It goes for the missions."

Bill climbed into bed. Dave lit a single candle as Bill watched. Their parents' voices, awkward and unhappy, drifted upstairs to where they sat and watched the candle.

"If Mom and Dad get a deborse," said Bill, "that would be a mortal sin." He didn't make much noise, but Dave could tell he was crying. He pulled the tabernacle curtain solemnly aside and fished out another candle. Gravely he lit it. With great care he placed the second candle beside the first, closed the curtain.

"It'll be okay."

By morning the last leaves were gone, stripped away by rain. In a week it was winter.

*

Ode to Snow

by William de Saint-Victor Swan, Esq.

Snow is good to hide in for a mouse:
Your brother likes it cause he makes his forts:
You play in it and must keep on your mitts:
You never play in snow if you have shorts.

Watch out when you are throwing snow:
A certain person can get very mad:
Then he will jump on all your books and papers too:
And mash them up quite bad.

*

Snow drifted deepest on those broad plains beside the river. The road out of Rigaud to Alston Vale was now a passage deeply cut through snow. Sometimes a skein of snow blew overhead from bank to bank, a veil flicked across the sun.

Today a black Chrysler beetled along this pale blue trench, headed for Como. In the back seat rode Léopold-Anatole. He liked to ride, pitying the world lavishly, bouncing softly past life's travails in a snug cocoon of heat. Soon the mansions of Hudson Heights appeared. On they creaked into Hudson, out the other side, into Como.

"I hope you will not be offended," said Léopold-Anatole in the hall of Como House, "when I tell you that I have come on an affair of business."

"We shall try to bear it," Nini assured him.

Before a portrait of the sisters' father, he paused. "He was a hero of the region," he pronounced firmly, before passing into the sitting room with a stern look and accepting a glass of wine. "The Glorious Goliath," he asked, a little distracted by the appearance of the liquid he now held, "*ça marche?*"

"We have got a contract to plough the station yard," said Nini.

"*Bouff*," he remarked, or it might have been "Baff." Plainly, the station yard of Como was not the rock upon which Léopold-Anatole proposed to have his clients build their church.

"*Tenez*." He fished out a document, studied it for a moment, laid it flat. "*Bon*, your father was my friend, and so I am your friend." He raised his glass as if to drink, sniffed it, put it back.

"Is that the plum?" demanded Nini with a sharp glance at Eleanor.

"The cranberry," said Eleanor. "I thought it was ready."

"Sometimes," continued Léopold-Anatole, determined not to founder on the wine, "one's political connections are useful in the matter of locating suitable—how do you say—works?" He opened his small, fat hands to show where such works were to be placed once they had been found. "Now is such a time."

And so the thing was done. A nod became a wink; a wink, a contract. A little ink was scribbled; the scribble witnessed; the business sealed and put away.

"And how do we repay this kindness?" asked Nini, as the last documents disappeared.

Léopold-Anatole was mortified. "Repay?" he choked. "But, how can one speak of this? I was an idolator of your father. It is the right word, idolator?"

"I begin to think so," admitted Nini.

Nevertheless, a payment formula was found that did not offend Léopold-Anatole. Certain sums would tiptoe out of one account and quietly appear in another. Sometimes these shy emoluments would bypass the books of Glorious Goliath altogether, making their way by night from who knows where. No Chinese mandarin was ever more discreet, nor ever mastered more back passages where the velvet-slippered feet of currency might pass unheard.

In the hall, Léopold-Anatole stopped at a portrait of a grandee of the old regime. Well had the artist caught that heavy pride which had dragged a handsome face into a permanent sneer. Even now the impasto seemed to breathe disdain.

"It is the Marquis de Vaudreuil," said Léopold-Anatole, drawing himself up in this august presence. "A great man of our nation."

"A vain and selfish aristocrat," said Nini, "and the ruin of his countrymen."

Léopold-Anatole sighed at these peccadilloes. "They were other times."

*

Nick and Dave constructed a labyrinthine snow-fort. They tunnelled into the yards-high bank thrown up by ploughs along Main Road. Soon a network of passages linked a hive of round blue rooms. Slot-thin adits wormed past trunks of buried hedges, turned, dashed out to sunlight for a breath of air, or dove into bluer depths.

As the fort grew, so did the corpus of its law. Childhood, that pitiless legislature, poured a stream of regulation into those muffled halls. Bill and Margaret learned there was scarcely a move they could make that did not flout some statute of the fort. When Ian Curry refused to grovel for a password, and tried to carry the portal by a *coup de main*, Nick and Dave scrambled for iced snowballs from a secret magazine. Ian was savagely repulsed. He fled crying, holding a hand to his face.

"We hit him in the eye," said Nick.

"He broke the law."

"What if he's blind?"

"Ian Curry is an asshole."

"I like your boots."

"Yes," said Dave, "only the rarest sealskin can be used, the skin of the silver seal." The boots had belonged to Rufus. Laced, they came to Dave's knee. The toes had been stuffed with newspaper to effect a fit.

"Dave," said Nick, "you never said anything about the bean-bread."

"It was a long time ago."

"You never said anything, like if you liked it."

"It made us fart," admitted Dave.

"David Swan!" cried Nick, and rushed from the fort in a rage.

*

At home a new writ ran among the Swans. Elaborate, careful, stiff, this covenant appeared as if proclaimed. Its chief rule was obliquity. Except for Noel, they spoke in parables of grief. Christmas came and went in a cloak of symbols now so charged with anguish that Lucy sometimes felt she could not breathe. Like children in a pageant, the boys played out their antique roles of sons at Christmastime. Bill was the only one who sometimes broke the rules.

"I don't think it's good for a father to be in an attic too much."

"Fathers have to work things out," Dave replied that time. "Fathers are not perfect all the time."

"Only the Supreme Bean is perfect."

"You never shut up about those nuns," snapped Dave, and stormed away.

Lucy adopted cheerfulness, while a skyful of tears waited behind her eyes.

"Well," she asked Bill, "what did you learn today?"

"God is our real father."

"That's nice."

"You're not even listening," said Bill glumly.

"You said God was our father," said Lucy. "They mean that figuratively, Bill. Your real father is your dad." Her voice came up on the last word.

They moved like figures at an oriental court, taut with etiquette. Dave began to treat Noel with shy formality, sometimes standing when his father came into a room. Bill resumed his table-setting duty, a task he had dropped a year before as only fit for kids.

"Forks on the left," he recited to Lucy as he seized a handful of silver from a drawer. "Dessert spoons at the top. Knife on the right." And he marched into the dining room.

"Thanks," called Lucy, too loud. "Sorry," she said, making it worse.

"And the little spoons go at the bottom," said Bill, "because it forms a pattern pleasing to the eye."

"Why not," said Lucy.

"Some nun gave him that pleasing-to-the-eye crap," grumbled Dave. "I can't do anything with that kid." Lucy took his arm and held it until he looked at her.

"You're okay, Dave."

"I'm not mad at anybody," he told her, gulping down his misery, swallowing it so it would not swallow him.

*

Noel became a legendary bungler. A kind of ghastly surgery trailed his blade as he bucketed through slumbering villages on Glorious Goliath's errands. All this he accomplished with a steadfast cheer that somehow retained its shape. Noel knew he was a rotten craftsman.

"I thought Curry was going to give up on that lawsuit," said Nini, "but now you've torn his hedge clean out."

"I'm not very good at things."

"Oh, balls," she muttered. Eleanor was scratching at a pad of figures. Nini shoved Noel into a chair. "What about a drink?"

"You bet."

"Just like Rufus," said Nini when she gave him a glass, "aim you one way, off you go the other."

"Dad?" said Noel.

"Bulls in a china shop, the pair. You butting about with your bloody machine; Rufus with his alligator and his dynamite."

"She starts drinking quite early now," said Eleanor without looking up. "Straight out of bed and into the booze."

"Not bad, this gooseberry," said Nini. "*Excellent* with cereal."

"Maybe I am a little like him," said Noel.

*

One time the alligator took a heron. Jumble of little bumps drifting across the pond towards that ash-grey bird where it stilted through the grass, eyes cocked for frogs, javelin beak laced to a whipsnap neck. Slowly along the shore it clocked its measured way while that drift of watching eyes eased through the water.

"Dad, we could have saved that bird," thinks Noel now, master of all this memory, prisoner, guiding it through stages or being led, remembering his father's face, Rufus so rapt as he witnessed the advance of time upon that execution.

"Dad," whispered Noel then, hardly more than a breathed word, an infusion of spirit into and against that gathered, watchful gallery of green. Rufus for answer gripped his arm in warning. They waited. It might have been a pair of acorns floating there, closing by lengths of leaves—that slow—upon the heron. Nothing in that bird's bright, water-piercing eye alerted it to coasting eyes.

Nothing alarmed its radar to that gliding shoal of teeth. In one brown, tail-driven lunge the snout broke water and attacked. Throwing grey wings aloft the bird fell back, dumbfounded, stained with flying mud. The lizard grunted, snapped again, and pushed back out from shore. Dragged out from shore that flopping mass of plumage, that frantic, ruined head, down into mud.

*

Nick began to ponder a new recipe. The breads, she decided, were not a success. Skeptical about the possibilities offered by her mother's slender library of cookbooks, she determined to improve whatever she found. She settled on a tuna casserole. High in protein.

First she assembled the ingredients, piled them into a bowl, and beat the whole mess into a suitable consistency, in this case the texture of fresh asphalt. This promising compound she improved with figs left over from Christmas. Dave came from an ancient line, she reasoned, so he would appreciate figs. She smoothed all this into a casserole dish and bounced it into the oven. Then she waited.

Inside half an hour the oven began to emit a stench which even love could not deny. Nick fished out her casserole, pitched it into the garbage without regret. She must find another route to Dave.

Drawn to a window, she pondered the Swans' house, an angular mansion rising from snow into a scheme of bay windows, an upper storey as high-ceilinged as the first, a roof that dodged about among gables.

"I will be beautiful for Dave," she vowed. Searching out a pair of scissors, she headed upstairs. In a closet hung her mother's wedding dress. She set to work.

*

A genius for figures revealed itself in Eleanor. Now she flung herself straight from bed upon whatever scraps of data she could find. Nothing was too trivial. The merest speck would be seized, marched to a column, multiplied, divided, pushed about until it yielded a fraction more of profit, an extra can of gas, a slight advantage, an hour of time, two hours, a week, another truck.

"You have become a slide rule," Nini remarked disconsolately as she shuffled past on her way to the kitchen.

"Just a coffee, darling," Eleanor said distractedly. "Black."

"At least Father always started with a drink," Nini said from the hall, slumping onto a bench and contemplating her slippers. "Generally he would take a little sherry, or a sniff of cognac. Nothing vulgar. *Then* he had his coffee."

"Thank you," said Eleanor, "not *too* strong, darling."

"He was a gentleman. He *resorted* to business; he did not *embrace* it."

"I think I'm onto something here."

"I shall have a drink," Nini proclaimed in a dull voice, "and then I shall fling myself upon that godlike boy." It was a speech without conviction, delivered to the floor and her slippered feet. "It would *disgust* Father," she added, rousing herself, "to learn that his children were plodding off to work each day as if they were a pair of mules."

But Eleanor plugged on, and Glorious Goliath grew, shed its skin, grew again. It threw its coils round this job, that, another still. Finally it was, withal, a force, and even so silken a plotter as Léopold-Anatole found himself amazed.

"We are ready for the larger works," he announced one afternoon, "works more lustrous. It is the right word, lustrous?"

"Balls," growled Nini, already drunk.

"If you mean the Seaway," said Eleanor, "then, yes, we are ready for the Seaway."

And so the trucks and graders, the belching Cats of Glorious Goliath, sallied out to help in the great work of gutting a river, of building dams, of opening a continent to ships.

"Just the place for Noel," Eleanor observed, inspecting a large map of the Seaway project. "It won't matter what he bumps into, it's all got to come down."

*

Margaret trudged through waist-deep snow, dragging a sled with her latest gift for Bill. This time her cargo was a hand-painted chair, frail in appearance, of a type that Helen Curry liked to buy at auction for large sums. Somehow Margaret had lashed it aboard and hauled it all the way. Curly huddled beneath the chair, regarding with plain horror that expanse of snow. Lucy met them at the kitchen door.

"Your mother isn't going to like this, Margaret."

"It's for Bill."

"You've got to stop looting your place."

"Mommy said I could give it to Bill."

"You're not fibbing, are you, Margaret?"

"She said I could."

Lucy knew she would have to insert the chair into a regular shuttle of goods that now carried Margaret's plunder back to her parents' house.

"I don't want her stupid chair," Bill whispered on the kitchen stairs.

"Have you seen her pussy yet?" demanded Dave.

"I don't want her stupid pussy."

*

"How will you get home?" asked Lucy.

"They have places to stay near the villages," said Noel. "I won't be coming home except weekends." Lucy looked at her hands, let them fall to her sides, looked helplessly around the kitchen. "It's best," said Noel.

"Sure," said Lucy. "I've never even heard of those places."

Noel grinned. "Don't worry. They'll be gone soon, anyway."

"You just destroy them?"

"They move them. That's what I'm told. I don't know. I guess I'll find out."

"I packed you a lunch," she said.

"Sure," said Noel, "thanks."

"There's a thermos of soup. It'll be freezing there."

"I know."

"You've never had to put up with anything like that."

"I can handle it."

Lucy nodded, her lips tight. She hauled out the thermos and checked to make sure its cap was tight, put it carefully back. "I guess I'll have to write my bar admissions."

"Sure," said Noel.

"You're not really here at all." She seized a towel, twisted it in her hands, held it against her. "You've changed too much."

"I know," said Noel.

"It's broken my heart," she whispered.

They heard a large truck shift down and brake to a stop at Charlie's lane. An airhorn sounded.

"I'd better go," said Noel. "I've got to load the Cat."

"Are you happy at least?" asked Lucy with tears in her eyes. "I mean, are you *going* to be happy?"

"I don't know."

Dave came into the kitchen when Noel left, stood by Lucy, watched his father walk away. "I hate that bulldozer."

Lucy ran a hand through his hair. "I didn't realize you'd got as tall as me."

"It's easier to be a kid," said Dave resentfully.

"You think it's easier for Bill?"

"I hate everything, so I don't care."

*

Ode to the Squirrel

by William de Saint-Victor Swan, Esq.

The squirrel is a furry fellow:
And he stays at home:
E'en in winter he finds some nuts:
And lo! he would not roam.

He fills up little pouches:
In his cheeks:
You cannot tell how many nuts he has:
Unless a person peeks.

They are an admirable beast:
And never shirk:
They know that somebody has to get up:
And go to work.

He is a lower vertebrata:
And ne'er doth make a fuss:
He does what the Supreme Bean wants him to:
Not like us.

*

Sister Agatha was gone, felled by a final Christmas and already missed. Old, wrathful, she had been reassuring too, and known. Her system with the pictures had been simple. On a material plane they were compensation for being struck by Sister Agatha. This was never much of a blow, and the children considered the bright cards an excellent reward. Some of these—the ones with gold trim—were prized. Many made their way into the equally devotional world of bubble-gum hockey cards, where Our Lady of Lourdes with a gold halo might fetch as high a price as a pair of Rocket Richards.

On a supernatural level the pictures gave equal value. By simply uttering what was printed overleaf, you earned an indulgence. This was always spelled out in concrete terms. "Jesus, Mary and Joseph," not a difficult incantation, earned three hundred days' reduction of whatever term of purgatory might eventually be handed down by the Last Judge. Children appreciated this edge, as who would not?

That regime was dead, fallen with Sister Agatha herself. A new power sat enthroned this term: Sister Mary of the Lamb of God. Young, freckled, straight, tall. From her came, not pictures, but perfectly blank squares of white cardboard.

"Keep these perfect and white, children, like the souls of those who do not sin," lectured Sister Mary of the Lamb of God in a high clear voice.

"Piss," whispered Sally.

"That's a venial sin," Bill told her.

"Who is that boy who spoke?" demanded Sister Mary of the Lamb of God.

"Bill Swan," chanted Sally.

"Come here, William," said the nun. Bill obeyed. "Give me your card, William." Bill complied. Sister Mary of the Lamb of God dug a card punch out of her habit and punched Bill's card. "Children must not speak, William, unless they are told to speak. So now you have a hole in your lovely card. It represents a sin."

Bill stared at the card in horror. Trembling, he returned to his seat.

"Piss," whispered Sally. This time Bill said nothing.

*

"You one of those political contracts?" the engineer asked.

"I just drive the Cat," said Noel.

The man shrugged and shoved the contract document into a pocket of his anorak. Behind him stood a yellow trailer mounted on blocks. Coal smoke rose through a black tin pipe. A grid of streets scored some empty fields nearby. There was no trace of farms. Gone were fences and silos, houses and barns.

"This is New Town Number Two," said the engineer as they surveyed the bleak landscape, "about as close to

Mars as you can get and still breathe air."

"You bet," said Noel.

A house began to appear from the direction of the river, first a roof, then a pair of dormers. Slowly the rest of the house heaved into view. Finally he could make out the lumbering frame that carried it along.

"Company from New Jersey," said the engineer. "They jack up the house, back that thing under it, and just drive away. Owner doesn't even have to pack the china."

"And you put it down here?" said Noel. "You move the whole town?"

"Six villages. They all go. Except the brick buildings. Brick buildings we burn and bulldoze."

"How do people feel?"

The engineer shrugged. "Not much fun to see your town get wrecked."

"Have they tried to stop it?"

"The sheriff comes in with an order. Not much they can do."

Three streets away they were backing the house onto its new foundation. A damp wind scoured the townsite. A couple watched, holding hands.

*

"Lucy?"

"Hi, Clem," said Lucy into the phone.

"Can I pop over?"

"I'll make tea," said Lucy. She'd been expecting the call. Lonely, she was glad it had come. She watched Clementine plough through the snow between their houses.

"You've been avoiding me," said Clementine as she shook off her snowy coat. "You are hiding."

"Why didn't you take the path?" asked Lucy, banging snow out of Clementine's galoshes. She turned them upside down over the register to dry. "I never hide," she added.

Clementine kissed her. "You *always* hide."

"I'm out of milk."

"I don't want bloody tea anyway," barked Clementine as she padded into the living room and occupied a chair. "Where do you *get* this furniture?" she wondered aloud, fingering the frayed material.

"How about brandy?" asked Lucy from the dining room.

"Isn't that a bit powerful?" said Clementine. "We're not exactly stranded in the Alps."

"I have sherry."

"Brandy will be fine." And when she had her glass: "We're not close, are we, Lucy?"

"No, Clem."

Clementine sipped at the brandy. "I'm afraid you'll think me rather nosy."

"I already think you're nosy, Clem."

"What are you going to do?"

"Law. I have the degree anyway. All I need is to write my bar exams."

Clementine scratched at the worn fabric and scowled. "I mean right now." She glowered around the room. "You are going to lose your lovely house."

Lucy sighed. "I think it's inevitable." Suddenly Clementine started to cry. Lucy crossed the room and knelt beside her chair. "We'll be all right," she told her. "And if we're not, you can paint a big, soulful picture of me and the children huddled in the snow."

"Lucy," sniffed Clementine, "I forbid you to make a joke of this. I want to help you."

"This is helping, Clem."

"I am *sagging* with money," said Clementine fiercely. "I have much more than Bud."

"We have plenty of money," Lucy said firmly.

Clementine dried her tears. "I'm a fool. We really are helpless."

"You mean, helpless over men?"

"Yes," said Clementine quietly, "it's what I meant."

"Of course."

"You'll let me help," said Clementine. It was spoken like an order, but both knew it was a plea.

"I don't think so, Clem."

*

"We do not need help from anyone," Dave announced to Lucy at dinner. "We are Swans."

"Were you eavesdropping, darling?"

"We are Swans," repeated Dave, and would not say more. After that, he sat in Noel's chair.

"Dave will be our dad," said Bill.

*

"I guess it's pretty hard with your dad gone," said Nick.

"Sure." They sat in the fort, in an indigo cave. Dave wore a magnificent cashmere topcoat, once Rufus's. A linen handkerchief sparkled in the breast pocket. He had opened the coat so Nick could squeeze inside.

"You have a lot of responsibilities, Dave."

"I must bear my family's name, even with the stain of dishonour."

"I will be *proud* to bear your family's name!"

"Sure."

Nick unzipped her jacket. "I have prepared my trousseau," she whispered. "This is only part of it." A white satin ribbon edged with lace ran around the collar of Nick's sweater, held there by rough stitches.

"It's beautiful," Dave told her earnestly.

"It's from my mother's wedding dress. She got it from my grandmother."

"It is an heirloom of the proud Jackson family," Dave pronounced.

"Yeah," said Nick, "only, my mother wasn't Jackson."

*

"How do we know that the Holy Father, when speaking *ex cathedra*, is infallible in matters of morals and doctrine?" asked Sister Mary of the Lamb of God. The children looked blankly at her. "Did Sister Agatha not get as far as the doctrine of infallibility?" she asked. There was no reply. "Sally?" Sally stared at her desk.

"We got as far as mortal sin," said Bill, "and how to add."

"Come up here, William," said Sister Mary of the Lamb of God. "Is your name Sally?" she enquired when he stood before her desk. The class giggled. "Did I ask you to speak?"

"I thought you wanted to know," said Bill.

Sister Mary of the Lamb of God smiled, fished out her punch, put another hole in Bill's card.

"Why did I do that, William?"

"Because you hate me."

Sister Mary of the Lamb of God punched another hole in Bill's card.

"That's one hole for talking out of turn, and one hole for thinking that I hate you. I don't hate you. I love all God's children. Now go back to your seat and be silent. You are getting a lot of sins on your card."

"The Supreme Bean would not pick on a kid," said Bill.

"God is not a vegetable," said Sister Mary of the Lamb of God. The class giggled. "Supreme *Being*," she corrected, punching another hole in Bill's card.

"He loves us," said Bill in a shaking voice.

"Nuns are married to Jesus Christ Our Lord," said Sister Mary of the Lamb of God, her face red. "So I don't think there is very much that an ignorant child can tell a nun about God."

"God's mother would not like a little kid to get too many holes in his card," said Bill. There were tears in his eyes. "She would not think it was fair."

"What do you know about God's mother, you blasphemous child?" yelled Sister Mary of the Lamb of God. No one giggled. "How dare you defy me?" She punched another hole in Bill's card, and another. There was no room left for more. She glared down at Bill from her own height and the added elevation of the dais. One fist was clenched, the other tightened around her punch, clicking it again and again. "Take your seat!"

"The Supreme Bean suffered little children to come unto him," said Bill through his tears. "He did not hit them or punch their cards."

"Sit down!" howled Sister Mary of the Lamb of God.

*

An hour after noon, already the snow was laced with thin blue shadows. Gus and Lucy sat on the swing in this frangible, dwindling light, blowing puffs of breath, watching their own joint shadow, grotesque and huge, slide back and forth across the snow.

"Your home is falling apart pretty fast, eh, Luce?"

"I guess it is, Dad."

They rocked for a while, content not to speak, cradled in that lulling swish of swing through snow.

"How soon before you can write your bar admissions?"

"Spring."

A clump of snow fell from an overhead bar into Gus's lap. He scooped a handful and examined it. "So you'll practise in Ontario. You're going to leave Noel?"

"He's left us." She watched her shadow navigate the snow, flashing along its contours, pausing before it rushed back. "We loved him, and now he's gone. I held him every night, and now there's nothing to hold."

"Pretty sad," said Gus.

"Boy," sniffed Lucy, "am I ever getting to hate that word."

From out on the frozen lake came the sound of a snowmobile. They turned to watch it, relieved, ready to draw what breath they could from that intrusive moment. It was large, almost the size of a bus, bright red with portholes in its sides. It roared over the brilliant surface, into their corner of day, and out. Into its wake fell the motion of the swing.

"You seem to be taking it pretty well."

"No," said Lucy, "I cry a lot. I'm just not crying now."

"Would you come and live with me?"

She shook her head. "I don't think we could do that. I don't think you could, either."

"Don't be silly," said Gus, anger in his voice.

She touched his arm. "I don't mean to make you mad."

"It's helplessness."

"I'm a big girl, Dad."

"And the boys?"

Lucy laughed. "Haunted by lovers. We need a Greek playwright around here." She shook her head. "Poor Bill. He's so damn gallant."

*

"I want that supple form to rush against me," said Nini, already a little gone at eight o'clock in the morning. "I desire *collision*." She watched with binoculars from an upstairs window, tracking Yves. "Suddenly I understand how atoms flatten when they hurtle out of tubes. I understand adherence." She reached, not even looking, for her wine. "I should have been a physicist." Yves toiled away with a snow-shovel, blowing breaths as big as clouds into the magnified field of Nini's lens. "Or possibly I mean physician."

"We must get more bulldozers," said Eleanor.

"My loins *howl* for the boy," Nini murmured against the glass.

"I don't say we ought to buy them," Eleanor muttered, "but lease them."

"Is this the *bloody* gooseberry again?"

"What?" said Eleanor. A pair of black-framed spectacles focused her search through the hectic terrain of her calculations. "You know,"—she tapped a foolscap tablet dense with figures—"Yves's father was going to pay us $11 an hour to widen that approach to the ferry dock."

"He is a churl," said Nini.

"The Seaway pays us $23."

"Dave Swan came by," Nini remembered all at once. "I meant to tell you. Wants to visit Noel. Wearing one of those outlandish scarves of Rufus's. Bit of a lord, that boy."

"We shall play the spread," said Eleanor. "We shall hire them in at $11, and out at $23."

"I told him we'd arrange it. For him to visit Noel, I mean."

"You know," said Eleanor, "I think we may become millionaires."

"We shall have to present a pair of pigs to the church, I suppose," said Nini absently. She groped for her glass. "Or a stained-glass window: Yves in a loincloth with his foot planted on my belly."

"It was Yves's idea, really," said Eleanor.

"Yves!?"

Nini was stung by this news. It made her feel ridiculous, a child. She wandered back to the window. Yves was no longer about. "What *is* this toxin?" she growled into her glass; but Eleanor was already back at work, hiring for less what she would soon rent out for more.

And so it was that Glorious Goliath's gravitational force, at one time barely enough to pull an apple from a tree, began to winkle out bulldozers from hamlets throughout Quebec. Soon a stream of machinery was arriving at the Seaway in the fresh, bright colours of its new mistresses, the one bent to her figures with a will, the other scouring her cellar for the plum.

*

Here comes the day of reckoning, rolling in under an ochre sky loaded with trouble. Playing the part of lead monster is Sister Superior, snatched from the farm as a rosy lass and polished over thirty years into this figure of spotless wardenhood: a plain ring wedded her to Christ; the sacred heart of Jesus glittered on her board-stiff bib. From tidy, weedless landscapes on the wall Our Lady gazed in vacant resignation, averting her eyes from the black strap that lay dead centre on the desk.

To Bill the principal looked like death herself. His heart beat terribly and his face felt hot. He stared at Sister Superior. Her mouth looked wide enough to swallow children whole. The wire frames of her glasses emerged so stiffly from her coif that they might have been screwed right into her skull.

Among the hardened criminals paraded in for punishment, Bill was the only one from his class. The others were older, all boys, all French. Sister Mary of the Lamb of God accompanied Bill; a thin, sour nun marshalled the others. One by one they marched forward to Sister Superior's desk and surrendered their cards. Sister Superior totted up the holes, yanked the offender forward by a wrist, and laid on. The sound petrified Bill. His face grew hotter and tears piled up behind his eyes. Sister Superior worked her way through the seasoned criminals. Mostly they took their strapping stoically, although one whimpered at the last blow. Bill's turn came. Sister Mary of the Lamb of God pushed him forward.

"He is young," observed Sister Superior.

"But very bold, Mother," said Sister Mary of the Lamb of God.

“He have seven holes?” She spoke precisely, delivering her English slowly.

“Yes, Mother.”

“Is too many.”

Bill stared at the strap. It was fat, covered in leather and roughly stitched. Here and there a wad of stuffing squeezed out between stitches.

Sister Superior sighed. “Come here, William.”

Bill froze. He could not move. He gaped at the strap. Sister Mary of the Lamb of God pushed him forward and this time Sister Superior took his wrist. Bill watched his hand in terror. Sister Superior brought the strap down once.

“Enough,” she said.

“But Mother,” protested Sister Mary of the Lamb of God, “he has seven holes.”

“Enough,” said the older nun angrily, scowling at her subordinate. Bill stumbled out. Dave waited with his coat.

“Come on, Bill. It’s okay.”

“I hope you will tell your parents that William has been disciplined for his behaviour,” said Sister Mary of the Lamb of God.

“My father’s a lawyer,” said Dave to the nun.

“I don’t think we need to worry about that,” said Sister Mary of the Lamb of God. “Not any more.”

“Come on, Bill.”

“I wet my pants, Dave.”

“It’s okay.”

*

“She said they were sins,” Bill said.

“I wonder what they eat,” said Lucy. “I mean the

nuns." She was standing on a chair craning to see into a high cupboard. "I wonder who does their shopping."

"Well, nuns are married to God. They probably get delivery."

"It would be nice if they could arrange to have a few things thrown in for us while they're at it."

"Probably you have to be married to God."

"I know I had some rice."

"We ate it," Bill told her. "We eat everything you buy when you buy it. If you bought more we could have a storehouse. We could put a lock on it and Dave wouldn't be able to throw any of it out."

"Did he throw out the *rice*?" said Lucy from the cupboard.

"I told you. We ate that rice."

"Shit," said Lucy.

"They'd give you forty holes for that," said Bill.

Lucy came down a step. She put a hand to her head, as if trying to recall something she had forgotten. Then she looked at Bill.

"Did someone hit you?"

"They gave him the strap," said Dave, coming into the kitchen.

"Did you throw that rice out?" demanded Lucy.

"We ate most of it."

"You threw *some* out, didn't you? I had some up there in that top cupboard."

"It's grown by slave labour, Mom. We shouldn't eat it."

"Damn! You make me so mad, Dave, I could wring your neck."

"They are paid fifty *cents* for a whole day's work!"

"Did you say they gave Bill the strap?"

"Bill's teacher is a cunt, Mom. She punches holes

in a little card. Later they add up the holes and give you the strap."

"Don't say 'cunt', Dave. It's a terrible word."

"It comes from Middle Low German. It's in the dictionary."

"I don't care if it's in the god damn Bible," snapped Lucy. "I am telling you I find it offensive. So cut it out."

"They would give him a hundred holes for cunt," said Bill.

"Let's see your hand," said Lucy. The welt was still visible. Lucy bit her lip. "Who did that, Bill?"

"Sister Superior."

"Why?"

"I had seven sins on my card."

"Bill was the only little kid in there," said Dave. "Sister Agatha never did that."

"She hates me," said Bill.

"Who does?" asked Lucy.

"Sister Mary of the Lamb of God."

"That broad is a shitbag, Mom," said Dave.

"Dave," said Lucy, "I think we could put shitbag on the list too, if you don't mind."

"She is a sack of steaming excrement."

"Fine. I know when I'm beat."

*

Construction of the seaway continued, canals and locks, bridges and power dams chewing their way steadily up the valley of the St. Lawrence. Noel was at ease in this.

One day they wrecked the village of Mille Roches. Its frame houses had already moved to New Town Number Two. Now it was time to burn. Men came in with gasoline.

They gutted with fire whatever was made of brick: some shops, a couple of houses, the two-roomed school. They dynamited what was left. Instead of a village, a street of smoking rubble straggled through a countryside of filthy snow.

No villager protested. None was angry. Arc lamps illuminated the church that night. They had taken the cross from its steeple; prised out its windows where their families' names were written in glass; carried this away. All around had been bulldozed clean. The church stood as if on a scaffold, awaiting death. They blew it apart, shoved it flat, erased it from the earth.

Throughout all this, Noel's world enlarged. That massive scale of sadness, the awful futility that scraped downriver under low, flat skies and rubbed away whole villages, seemed to erode his clumsiness until it fell away. Nothing about a big, ham-fisted man was awkward here. He grew into the place and lived inside its doom. His sympathy expanded on that devastated plain. Finding something large enough to love, he fit.

*

Gordon Curry decided to build a slide. Just like that. A single tic of delight had somehow twitched that haberdasher's soul, just once, and out had popped this single stone of craziness.

Gordon's slide was raised on succeeding layers of hard-packed snow, troughed to hold a toboggan, iced. It took three Allards a week to make. When it was done, and Gordon satisfied, it wound around his house like a glass channel and plunged a hundred yards to finish at the lake.

The slide signalled a truce, a kind of blanket remission of every grudge or feud that troubled Como. Everyone came. Eleanor and Nini draped themselves in outlandish sleighing robes, traipsed next door, and arrived at the starting platform. A knot of tobogganers surveyed the run.

"I had no idea you were so *raffish*," drawled Nini shamelessly. Gordon grinned.

"Come on, we'll take you down."

"*Absolutely* not," giggled Nini.

"*Dear* Miss Lofft," said Gordon in a tone of such revolting gallantry that Nini, in other circumstances, would have struck him for it. But no restraint, it seemed, was left in Como. Gordon took Nini's arm and settled her. Helen clambered on behind and seized Nini round the waist.

"Push!" commanded Helen, and Gordon shoved them off. They slid into the narrow trough and rocketed away. Nini's eyes bugged as they rushed into the first sharp turn. Surely no law of physics could hold that shrieking torpedo of wrapped arms upon the slide. But the turns had been engineered by masterful Allards. The ramp tilted, curled, and a load of hurtling womanhood threaded the course as though on rails.

"This is nuts," said Lucy when her own turn came.

"Push!" roared Helen, seizing this latest victim in her grasp and speeding off again.

For almost a week the Currys' slide united Como in a mania. Soon they were into time trials. The Allards made a toboggan of solid steel, iced the bottom, and almost tore the slide apart in their descent. Of course they took first prize. The slide's potential for personal glory emboldened everyone. Bill astonished Lucy by being the first to ride down backwards. Dave made it standing up.

Margaret strapped on a wretched, mewling Curly and shot him on his way. His red-tipped ears flicked once, pathetically, before they vanished round a bend.

This was how it went until a warm front moved up from the south and started nibbling at the ice. One afternoon Gordon took a hard look at the lake, where his outrun shot the riders at slide's end. He decided the ice was rotting, and ordered a halt.

Naturally the children disobeyed. Whenever they could, they snuck onto the slide and rode in a giddy spray of meltwater the whole way down. They were children, weighed not much, got away with it for a while.

Until the end of a run, on a billowy white day, when Margaret got off her short toboggan, still laughing, and turned for shore. She was only a few yards out when she stepped through soft ice and sank to her knees. There must have been a shelf or secondary layer of ice below. For a moment it held.

"Hey!" shouted Ian. Margaret just stood there, amazed, staring at him, up to her knees in slush. Finally whatever she was standing on gave way, and she was gone.

*

Margaret's death struck the village an ugly blow. That bond of enchantment, spun out of nothing by the magic of the slide, returned to nothing. Como became a village of averted eyes. Instead of joining them together, Margaret's death built walls of desperate perplexity, as if they had betrayed each other with some act of wickedness.

In spite of lengthening days the yacht club remained deserted. No one prepared his boat for spring. Those who were called to the club by duty—people with keys, committee men—seemed unable to regard the lake at all, and scarcely looked at each other.

Finally enough black water threaded the loosening ice to allow a boat to navigate. The men loaded ropes and hooks and took their seats without a word. On their way downstream they stared at their rubber boots, embarrassed by what they were about. On a swift spring current they swept past Quarry Point and through the Narrows, past Curry's point. They heaved in grapnels and began.

Each day those silent boatloads left the yacht club jetty, shot downstream on the flood. Each day they searched for Margaret farther off. No one in Como spoke of it at all. Women bought groceries and did not exchange a word. Men mumbled when they met.

When they found her a month later, the retrieval of that small body released the tension, first into tears. They buried Margaret, wept for a day or two. Then they erupted into turbulent relief. The yacht club rang like a fair ground. There was laughter in the street. Como danced a light, sweet step along its little shore, tossing its silly curls and raising its arms to spring.

Then the women rebelled.

Nini disappeared on a drunk, scooping a fistful of cash out of Glorious Goliath's receipts and heading into Montreal. Lucy began to pack her household into boxes: sort, classify, reject. In a fury she vandalized her past. Helen Curry took up boxing, started to train. She could be seen in the early morning jogging through lanes. In the afternoon, while Clementine and her gang of daubers squatted by some pile of slab, Helen would come storming down her lawn in a sweatsuit, take up position at a grey sack full of sand that hung where it could be seen, and whale away.

"Wah!" she gasped as she struck the punching bag,

"wah, wah, wah!"

Nick decided to leave her parents and move in with Dave. She was now fourteen and Dave thirteen, she declared, and she was not about to drift into spinsterhood because a bunch of grown-ups could not see that she longed for Dave, and he for her, and that was that.

"We are not a bunch of grown-ups," Bud told her with remarkable calm, "we are your parents."

"I'm outta here," said Nick.

*

Como trembled on the edge of lawlessness. A few more women caught the spirit of mutiny and began to send experimental sneers lapping at their husbands' chairs. There were some cold suppers. One or two men made their morning journey into Montreal in badly ironed shirts. A score of astonished children began to find their mildest complaints returned to them shredded by contempt. Finally this rising of women reached a peak, levelled off, fell away, its ranks thinned by a steady enfilade of custom, disillusionment, fatigue. Only its four originals remained entrenched, grasping what cudgels they had seized, changed for good.

Lucy.

Helen.

Nini.

Nick.

*

Margaret's death had uncovered something diamond-hard

in Nick. She was too big to push around, discovered this herself, and soon was slinging her gold-bright hair and swift, unyielding eyes as if they were a clutch of javelins. Bud and Clementine, with Lucy, decided to play along. Nick went stamping across to the Swans' with a bag of clothes.

"I'm putting you in with me," Lucy told her. "There's plenty of room and we'll have our own bathroom."

"What about Mr. Swan?"

"I don't think you have to worry about Mr. Swan for the moment."

"You're not going to talk me out of marrying Dave, Mrs. Swan."

"You can put your stuff in the bottom drawer, Nick, and there's plenty of space in the closet."

"Dave and I are in love. From now on he is my betrothed. We are flesh of our flesh and bone of our bone. Dave looked it up."

"You sleep in *my* room, Nick."

*

Helen ran. She contrived a series of looping routes that took her through the village and home again. Early commuters heading for morning trains would meet her chugging across lawns.

"That woman is *haunting* me," cried Clementine to Bud as they watched her pound by on her way down Charlie's road. "She has become a *wraith*."

It was true that this training obsessed Helen. No more did she bruise herself against Clementine's little group, but instead rampaged about on her errand of rage or grief, punching, running, wrapped in battle. She became thinner, quieter. She rarely spoke, and when she did was excessively polite. Clementine read this as a rebuke, and felt it keenly.

"I cannot bear it," she told Lucy. "Helen has become *remote*."

"Yes," said Lucy, who was not listening, had a passion of her own.

*

Lucy waded into her troubled life with a club of purpose, dragging it piecemeal from where it hid and dealing it hard clouts. Her chief assistant in this was Nick, who was everywhere: a toss of yellow hair, a thrash of limbs, eager to be Lucy's acolyte. Drawers were pillaged and closets searched, chests spilled onto sunlit floors. Spring came in through windows. Lucy prowled about deciding what should live, what die. She began to hum.

"How come you're singing, Mom?"

"I saw some lilies of the valley, Bill, under the cedars."

"Things are getting pretty messy around here."

"Stop whining, Bill," said Nick.

"And tulips," Lucy said.

Her fever drove her underground, into the twisting, many-chambered basement. Lucy usually dreaded this earthen space alive with spiders. First she opened a kitchen door and peered down. Later she went outside and unlocked a rotting portal that led in from ground level. She swung it back against the house and poked at some cobwebs with a stick. At last she stormed straight in.

"Boy! We could open a store with this junk," she yelled out to Bill.

"We could leave it there," called Bill, worried, watching Lucy's flashlight flicker from sight. "Mom?" Cool air blew out, smelling of dirt and damp cement. He heard snatches of Lucy's voice. A gust of wind lifted the heavy door, as if to shut it, before it fell back with a bang. "Mom!" Bill screamed, angry at Lucy for his fright.

"What's the matter?" Lucy struggled out with a dirty carton. Bill looked sullen and embarrassed.

"We don't need more junk, Mom."

"Exactly." She dropped her dusty cargo at his feet. "Haul that onto the lawn." Before Bill could protest, she'd gone back into the cellar for another box.

They had a bonfire by the lake: discarded furniture, curtains, pages of old words: all pitched into flames. Neighbours came by and watched. Some helped. Lucy, the boys, and Nick burned through one whole day, serving the skies of spring with notice that the Swans were ready for a change.

*

Nini began her dash at Como station, arriving with a satchel of currency to find all local trains had come and gone. Treating the stationmaster with feudal condescension, she bullied him into stopping the transcontinental on a pretext, and climbed aboard. Pressing some bills into a surprised conductor's hand, Nini went forward until she found a bar car. By the time those silver coaches drew into Windsor station—not long—Nini had begun her blistering run for freedom, and decided what to drink along the way: not the plum.

At the Ritz-Carlton she took a corner suite, commanded a fire to be lit, glared at Mount Royal for a while, and sent for dinner. Later she wandered outside, bumped along Sherbrooke Street in a press of springtime walkers. When she reached McGill University, she sat on a low stone wall. Her blood seethed with Scotch. She placed her hands flat against the cold stone, just to feel it. Lovers went by, pasted together by youth, by Montreal, and by a subterfuge of books. Night blew off the mountain, cold. Nini hailed a taxi and headed for that net of streets below Rue Notre-Dame, for its livid sneer of fake *auberges* and cellars alive with hands. She fetched up two nights later at a rooftop bar in New York; snapped into consciousness all at once; beheld a pair of anxious eyes, a blazer, parted hair, a sweet decrepit smile.

"I think you're a very special person," declared this sum of parts.

"We're together, then, are we?" said Nini.

"Ha ha," he answered nervously, one pink hand curled round a glass whose sides were stained with a bright, viscous residue.

"I don't suppose you've robbed me," mumbled Nini, rummaging around her person long enough to locate a wad of notes, examine it.

"You shouldn't wave money like that," trilled the blazer, gluing a choir-boy's smile onto his dried-out face, where it failed to stick, and started to come off in bits.

Nini yanked a promising chunk of bills from her wad and shoved them across to the bartender. "Give my friend here a tumbler of that nice fruit drink," she told him, "and if he tries to follow me, kill him."

*

Bill appeared one day with Curly. The cat slumped

indifferently from the child's arms, looking like some large, furred cell about to divide.

"They don't want him," Bill told Lucy, and this turned out to be true.

Bill constructed an elaborate bed for Curly. He expelled his books from their trunk and stuffed the space with cushions and blankets. When it was done, Curly's bed seemed to vie with Bill's altar for devotional pride of place. But Curly would have none of it. He shot one look at the statue of the Virgin crushing a snake with her bare foot, and padded for the back hall.

"It's okay," Bill tried vainly to assure the cat, "she's only plaster."

*

When Nini returned she demanded a job.

"Well," said Eleanor, clicking figures into a new machine, "it won't be much good if you just grab cash whenever you feel like it." A roar distracted them. Yves bounced through their gate on a small tractor, towing a flatbed trailer into the yard. A steel tank strained against cables that held it to the swaying trailer. "That's for diesel," said Eleanor. "We are going to wholesale it to ourselves. We discovered that Mr. Allard was robbing us."

"The Allards have been robbing us for generations," said Nini stiffly. "It is what they are *for*. It is what *we* are for."

"You may leave it to Yves and me."

"I shall *not*," vowed Nini. "Our sheds burst with yellow machines. I dine alone while you and Yves muster these objects."

Eleanor sighed. "You have no head for figures."

"Nonsense. There is more to business than figures."

Eleanor shoved her glasses onto her forehead and studied her sister. "We do have a weakness," she said doubtfully. "We are not as close to politicians as we might be. I fear we rely too much on Maître Gingras."

"Pay out the bribes ourselves, should we?"

Eleanor stitched a few more figures into her machine. The sisters waited as it chewed its way through. When it was done, Eleanor tore off the tape and pursed her lips.

"I believe it is known as government relations."

*

"Lise is going to kill Sister Mary of the Lamb of God," said Bill as they waited for the taxi.

"Good," said Dave, "that broad is the *numero uno* pain of all time."

"Lise could go to hell for it."

"Get real, Bill. They'll make her pope if she torpedoes that slut."

"What's a slut?"

Dave shrugged. "It depends on what kind of slut they are."

"Well, I think she would be the holy kind, because God married her."

"Wake up, Bill. They're just women. They like it when the male of the species has a boner."

"Boners are a sin. If you get a boner you could get the wrath of God the Father Almighty and of Blessed Mary, Ever Virgin."

"That Lamb of God cunt has got you spooked. I hope Lise takes her out with a Luger."

Thus absorbed in topics that ranged from theology

to ballistics, the brothers passed their time until the taxi arrived.

"Hello, Beel," trolled Lise, tugging him onto her lap with a hairy arm. "Beel, Beel, *c'est avril*," chanted Lise as the taxi swayed off down the road and Bill sank back into a comfortable world of wide legs, promised vengeance, and a strong smell of breakfast.

*

Noel drank a lot. He thought about a white house with a red tin roof, in sunshine above a sliding lake, and a silver steeple glinting on the farther shore. He would think this, and take a drink, and the pain that was freeing up his heart would be a little easier to bear.

He remembered the alligator's end, the smell of Charlie's truck on that last journey in, leading the other truck. Rufus never said a word. Alligator on the dam, a few chewed sticks nearby. They got him with ropes—they made it look so easy—and into the zoo's open truck. Imagine the alligator's leaden comprehension watching this rope descend, watching himself get lashed to a wooden floor. Feeling a hard smack of wood against a belly that liked to slide in mud. Imagine that journey away from the tranquil pond, his muddy empire and his unmindful subjects.

Rufus never saying a word.

*

"Dat Sister Lamb, she beat you up, eh, Beel?"

"She gives me a lot of holes," admitted Bill. The taxi

swayed along into Hudson. Lise held Bill firmly on her lap. Sometimes she rocked him, holding him gently against her and nuzzling his cheek.

"I give her one big hole herself, Beel," Lise muttered darkly. "I give dat sister a big hole to tink about."

"It's a mortal sin to kill a nun," said Bill, unable to envision any other end to an assault by Lise.

"De priest take care of dat sin, Beel," Lise whispered through a cloud of sausage, "and I take care of Sister Lamb."

"I think I talk too much," said Bill nervously. "I'm a talkative child."

"You okay, Beel," Lise said fiercely.

"Okay," said Bill.

*

"Does a venial sin require the intercession of a priest in order to be forgiven by God?" asked Sister Mary of the Lamb of God. Into a sea of perfect innocence sailed this question from the bride of Christ. Never before, the ranked countenances of children seemed to say, had a subject as alien as sin ever cut its barnacled keel through their virgin waters. A less suspicious heart might have been mollified by this angelic sight, but not the nun's.

"I am waiting," Sister Mary of the Lamb of God told them, although, for sure, they knew. On the blackboard behind Sister Mary of the Lamb of God were drawn three milk bottles. The first of these was perfectly white. The middle bottle was flecked with black, as if someone had scraped dried paint into otherwise pristine liquid. The last was black.

"Which bottle represents the soul sullied by venial

sin?" Sister Mary of the Lamb of God called impatiently. No answer. "Then we shall have to ask someone who ought to know. William?"

"Yes, Sister?" said Bill, too frightened to add more.

"I have asked a question, William."

"Yes, Sister."

"Are you too stupid to remember the question?" Someone giggled.

"Yes, Sister," said Bill. He was trembling.

"Which bottle, William, represents the soul sullied by venial sin?"

"The middle bottle, Sister."

"That is right, William. The middle bottle. Now, is it necessary to obtain the intercession of a priest in order to have a venial sin forgiven by God?"

"A priest is always a help, Sister," said Bill earnestly. "It would be good to have a priest."

"William,"—she smiled murderously—"we are not asking you to be a lawyer, as your father *used* to be. What we are asking for is a straight answer. Do you need a priest to forgive a venial sin?"

"Yes," said Bill, assuming, incorrectly, that to err on the side of authority was the safest course.

"No," said Sister Mary of the Lamb of God, and Bill got another hole.

*

Noel became more forgetful. Jobs went undone. That poor, sad serpent watched him from a vanished pond.

Dad.

Eleanor wanted to sack him, and a fight ensued between the sisters. Nini became enraged, called Eleanor a ledger, and demanded to know, in any case, what had become of the plum? In the end they hid Noel in one of Glorious Goliath's peripheral operations and life went on, not entirely as before.

*

On the front steps of the parish school of St-Thomas-d'Aquin, Fate rolled up her sleeves and looked for Sister Mary of the Lamb of God. That which the nun had sown she was about to reap. For a long time now, too long, a series of transgressions had dropped onto one side of the scales of justice, each one pinging into the pan with no more sound than, well, a venial sin. But they had added up: the scale had tilted at last, and here was come a clenched and meaty fist to set it right.

Bill made his way to the taxi, determined not to cry, his hands red from the latest totting up of holes. Sister Mary of the Lamb of God radiated a piety so dense that even Sister Superior wrinkled her nose in disgust.

"Cunt," said Lise, striding up to Sister Mary of the Lamb of God and planting herself before the startled nun.

"What, my child?" said Sister Mary of the Lamb of God.

"Beetch," said Lise, and ploughed her in the gut with a fist like a bag of rocks.

"Bwaaah," said Sister Mary of the Lamb of God.

"No more 'oles," Lise told her sternly, and stomped off to the taxi.

"Bwooorgh," said Sister Mary of the Lamb of God.

*

"I hear they expelled Lise," Lucy called from the pantry under the kitchen stairs. Lucy had selected this space for security reasons, provisioned it, installed a lock.

"Now she drives the taxi," said Bill.

"I thought I bought a whole case of that macaroni."

"It may not be there any longer."

"Is Lise old enough to drive a taxi?"

"She was too old for school," said Bill. "She wants to marry me."

"Shit!" said Lucy. Her head appeared in the pantry door. "Are you trying to tell me Dave threw out that macaroni?"

"The main food groups are listed in the Canada Food Guide," Bill told her. "You only get essential nutrients by choosing foods from the main food groups."

"That little prick," muttered Lucy.

"Mom!"

"How did he get in there?"

"He picked the lock."

She looked hopelessly into the pantry. "Lise hit that Lamb of God nun, didn't she?"

"They gave her the strap for a long time. She just laughed."

"How's that hole business going?" Lucy gave up her search and shut the pantry door.

"I don't get holes any more. I made a special devotion to the Blessed Virgin."

"How does that work?"

"You make your altar into a Blessed Virgin altar. You put up your picture of Our Lady of Perpetual Help, beside your statue of Our Lady Queen of Heaven."

"You think that's what worked?"

"I make special gifts. Anything from a child with an innocent heart that has been cleansed of the stain of original sin through the sanctifying power of the sacrament of baptism, and cleaned up later by the sanctifying power of the sacrament of penance, is especially pleasing to the Mother of God."

Lucy tugged open the fridge. "Did Dave dump that stew I had in here?"

"If a food like that gets too many micro-organisms in it, they will start to thrive," Bill explained. "They could take over your whole body."

"I could murder Noel for giving him those science books," said Lucy.

"Honour thy Father," said Bill.

*

"We'll be covered in mud," Dave warned.

"Don't worry," said Nick. "Parents expect you to be covered in mud. They never think it's because you went for a fuck."

"It's kind of awful to hear a girl use that word."

"Bullshit."

Pungent smells of sawdust and spring mud suffused the air. They slogged along in their rubber boots. Swallows flashed about the mill, patching old nests and plastering new ones into eaves. Sluggish green flies blundered about. Dave kicked at a ridge of sawdust that glinted with ice.

"The ice stays inside for a long time," he said. "Sawdust is an insulator."

"Big deal," said Nick.

"In the olden days that's how they kept ice frozen. They cut big blocks out of the lake and put them in special icehouses. They covered them with sawdust. It lasted all summer. People didn't have refrigerators."

"That's great, Dave."

Nick led the way under the mill. Spring vanished at a step. They entered a gloomy half-winter that lingered out of sight, a mess of ice and frozen mud. Nick went straight through to their room beneath the sawyer's booth. A ridge of ice had formed a high sill that partially blocked their way. They scrambled over this. It was so cold inside that neither spoke. They remained like that, intimidated by the suddenness of the cold, until Nick kissed him on the mouth.

"This time I want you to put your cock inside."

"Sure," gulped Dave. On the floor was a sleeping bag and Hudson's Bay blanket.

"I smuggled them in yesterday," said Nick.

"They'll get dirty."

"For crying out loud, Dave, did I ask you to help with the laundry? I mean, cripes, do you want to get laid or not?"

"Sure."

"Take your clothes off," she directed, slipping out of her windbreaker and hanging it on a nail. Dave climbed out of a vast, double-breasted blazer, folded it carefully, laid it on a beam, and stood demurely on the sleeping bag. Nick tugged off her sweater and flung it away. Dave stepped out of his pants. They lay down.

"Do you want me to suck your cock first?"

"What for?"

"I don't know," admitted Nick. "It's supposed to be good."

"There'd be germs."

"I guess so."

They burrowed into the sleeping bag together, surprised at the touch of each other's cold skin. They listened to the rush of wings outside, where the nesting swallows came and went a few feet from their hiding-place. A bee stumbled loudly by, patrolling the sunlit wall beyond their den. Water dripped loudly into the under-mill.

"I think you're getting a boner," said Nick.

"Yeah."

"You have to put it into my pussy."

"I know," said Dave heavily. "I hope you don't get a baby."

"Don't be stupid," she scoffed.

"I sure liked it when you had a trousseau and didn't have to be so bossy."

Constricted by the sleeping bag, he struggled into a kneeling position. Nick spread her legs as wide as she could.

"Your balls look funny," she told him.

"It won't reach," said Dave, holding onto his penis.

"Cripes, Dave. You're supposed to lie on top of me."

"Oh yeah." He fell forward.

"Ouf!"

"Is it good?" he asked.

"It's not even in." And later, "We'll have to get married, Dave."

"You walk in beauty."

"I know."

They faced each other, breathing into each other's faces. Beyond those fragile, ancient boards where the lovers made their nest, beyond their dreaming youth and their bright confused elation, went the black river.

*

"Dad will never come home," said Bill.

"He is casting himself upon life's seas," said Dave

from his atlas.

"Mom cries."

"I know."

"I try to comport myself with dignity."

"You do okay."

"Mom will have to be a lawyer to take care of us."

"She doesn't mind. A lot of people like being lawyers. Mr. Jackson likes it okay."

"Are you going to be a lawyer?"

"The Honourable Sir David Beaucourt Swan, Q.C., Attorney-General of Canada, appearing for the defence, m'lord."

"I thought you were going to be a space lawyer."

"The defendant is a Martian accused of murdering the Queen of Bees."

Dave's room was warm with lamplight. The brothers lay folded on the bed, flung limbs and old pyjamas, faces dreaming.

"Tell me about a country," said Bill.

"The country of the Queen of The Netherlands is small, though rich in floriculture and the production of cheese. Their royal family is the House of Orange-Nassau."

"And in their country," added Bill, "people like to stay with their kids."

*

Nini arranged that a truck would stop for Dave and take him to visit Noel. Dave prepared for the trip by dressing carefully in a white shirt, an Irish tweed jacket hacked down in size by a tailor in Hudson, an ascot scarf. When the truck arrived he climbed a ladder to the cab, rode off amazed that anything this high could be a truck. For an hour they made their way through farms, crossing the old seigneuries of Beaucourt and Saint-Victor, until they reached a plain and climbed the St. Lawrence.

Noel was waiting to meet Dave. He might have seen himself in this tall, nervous boy, had he been looking. But he was not, and his self-conscious grin, as of a shy man greeting a stranger, frightened Dave.

For a few hours they poked about, stiff, embarrassed. Noel showed Dave a collapsed village, asked after Lucy. Dave said "sure" and "fine" a hundred times. They parted wretchedly, relieved at least.

*

Noel drove into Wales, a bottle of gin between his legs. He took a deserted avenue, and another, loafing along in a pleasant cloud of booze and wickedly intoxicating air. Here came that swollen river, dragging whole mountainsides of melted snow and ruined vegetation out to sea. Sometimes a rack of antlers floated past, rotating slowly in the thick green flood. Here came a thousand gunports staring with cannon. Here came the British recklessly to test Montcalm, who lay along the Beauport shore awaiting Wolfe.

"Excellent!" cried young Lieutenant Swan that time they tried to carry the French position by main assault. Later they withdrew before a storm of musketry, took to their boats in reasonable order, properly bloodied by the French. Montcalm held Beauport, wrapped it in iron, and Wolfe, beset by illness and the steady drip of time, prowled round Quebec, leaden with despair.

Later came that clash of armies on a field in rain.

As a battle it was not much, except that it yielded a pair of heroes and a continent. It is this silt a river bears.

Swans inhabited this land of rivers like a genealogy of dreamers. Wrapped in a sparkling helix in their cells, some memory of rivers roamed their blood. None could hear unmoved the sound of water gliding over plains. It slid through nets of islands, rubbed past rocks, arrived where Noel lay swilling sunshine with his gin. Transfixed by the rushing current, he thought of Rufus and the alligator. That is how his epiphany appeared: bobbing along beneath a sky as bright as tin. Noel set out to buy paint.

*

News came to Como that Noel was painting fields.

"A field?" said Nini. "That darling boy."

"They do not like it," Léopold-Anatole said lamely. He shrugged and spread his hands, as if to show how much offence a field of paint might cause. "We shall have to sack Mr. Swan," he observed with sadness.

"Eh?" said Nini.

"Sack, it is not the right word?"

"We cannot sack him!"

"Not?" replied the lawyer.

"It might be necessary, you know," said Eleanor from a clenched face.

"You want to fire Noel?" exploded Nini. "Is this what we have become?"

Eleanor watched her sister frigidly. "We have become a business," she pronounced.

*

On the plain of the St. Lawrence a bright green tail began to grow. Its tip appeared in a combe a quarter-mile inshore, ran up a hill, broadened onto a stretch of abandoned tillage that bordered New Town Number Two. It was a tail of paint. Here it clung brightly to a stone or stem. It dripped from branches onto naked earth, where it lost its vividness, became suffused with loam, and retired into a memory of pigment. Children came to help, detecting a conspiracy.

*

"It might not be a good idea for us to move."

"Well, Bill," said Lucy, "I'm afraid it's the only idea I've got."

"I like it here."

"I'm not surprised. It's the only place you've ever lived." Lucy studied the opened fridge with a doubtful look.

"Curly doesn't pee on the altar any more."

"I'm a little afraid to ask what happened to the chicken I had in here."

"It's cruel to eat a chicken. They are slaughtered by barbaric means."

"I hope you guys have to support me some day."

"Mom, those chickens are still *alive* when they kill them."

"You've got me there."

"I will make a novena to Blessed Mary Ever Virgin, Mary Queen of Heaven, Our Lady of Sorrows, Our

Lady of Perpetual Help, Our Lady of Fatima, Our Lady of Lourdes, and Notre-Dame-de-Beaupré. I will make a new altar."

Lucy sat down, took Bill's hands, searched his serious face. "Do we need that, Bill? We already have a lot of blessings. I have you."

"We could ask for Dad to come home."

"I think we have to accept that Dad is doing what he wants to do."

"Maybe if he knows we won't make him be a lawyer."

"I'm going to do my best, Bill. I really am going to do my best."

"Children should be seen and not heard," said Bill.

*

"I have to have a boyfriend, Dave," insisted Nick.

"Ian Curry is a cocksucker."

"All I'm saying, Dave, is that when a man moves away, it's hard for a woman who has plighted her troth to keep it that way. I mean, for ever. She can keep troth for a few years, but then she has to get herself a man. It's the law of nature."

"Fuck the law of nature," muttered Dave.

"Everything you know about fucking, you learned from me," said Nick smugly, "so you don't have to keep swearing."

"I knew *tons* about fucking," said Dave vehemently. "What about the fallopian tubes?"

"The what?"

"See," he crowed. "I know more about the mysteries of the female body than you do, and you are the female of the species."

“This isn’t getting us anywhere, Dave,” said Nick solemnly. “We have consomméed our love. We need each other. I’m not going to become an old maid like the Loffts.”

“The Loffts have Yves to fuck.”

“Dave,” said Nick severely, “get serious. They are English and Yves is a Frenchie. They would never fuck him. It would lead to the bastradation of the races.”

They had climbed down a shattered patch of seawall to a tumble of boulders that lay at the base, half out of the rushing current. It was a favourite retreat. Swift, dark green, and cold, the lake slid by. They perched on warm stones, islanded.

“How far is Ottawa?”

“Not far,” said Dave. “About ninety miles.”

“Ninety miles!” cried Nick. “Dave, this doesn’t look good for us.”

“It’s not that far,” he said dejectedly.

“We’re kids, Dave. Even though we’ve consomméed our love and bear the secret of our plighted troth, we still don’t have a car.”

“If you go out with Ian, I’ll kick his nuts right up to his teeth.”

“You must really love me,” said Nick approvingly.

“I’ll kick his brains into paste.”

“He doesn’t have any brains,” said Nick.

“How come you want him for a boyfriend, then?”

“Dave—” her voice was heavy with exasperation. “I don’t *want* him. I just said I might *need* him.”

Oka clustered by the water on the far shore. Its steeple flashed in the brittle light. The ferry put out from its wharf and was snatched away by the current. They could hear the launch roar against the dragging water. It looked as if the ferry must snap its line and shoot downriver to Montreal. But finally the launch halted its downstream slide, turned into the current, and began to claw up to Como.

"If you visit me we could go to Rideau Hall," said Dave. "The Governor-General is Grampa's friend."

"The Governor-General is like the Queen," said Nick, impressed in spite of herself.

"Yes," said Dave.

Nick pondered this. "My dad is a Queen's Counsel."

"So is mine."

"Yeah," said Nick thoughtfully. "They're members of the bar and they're Her Majesty's counsel. That's how come they get to wear silk instead of ordinary robes."

"Ian's father sells shirts," Dave observed pointedly.

"Yeah," said Nick. "And socks."

*

Next the tail grew legs. It widened into a body, serrated on top, and sprouted these majestic limbs. They curled from beneath the reptilian belly, strangely powerful, ending in claws that pushed for a grip in the soft earth of fields. By now there was a regular crew of painters, children and some adults, who consulted gravely over each new joint or bit of scaly hide before they helped to rough it out and slop down paint.

Noel used any shade of green he could get. His little party of supporters split into fierce and eloquent factions, each one staking out some tint of viridescence for its own, defending it with high words against contesting hues. Throbbing viridian, Kelly green, the lofty silver sneer of sage: all of it went slapping across shoals of gravel, grass, the trunks of fallen trees. Viewing it all from high ground one day, Noel saw that spring was blurring the alligator's lines. Vernal green was attacking the coloured form like a thickening fog. A running squad of brush-thrashers was mobilized to hack away offending shrubs, and Noel began to outline his growing beast with brilliant strokes of yellow, blue, or even white.

In the course of easing Noel out of sight, Glorious Goliath had taken back its truck and given him another. Instead of the company's snappy livery, Noel's pickup was adorned with primer, rust, a lot of mud. In this brave vehicle he bucketed about the countryside collecting paint. At first the merchants robbed him blind. They sold off ancient stocks of paint. Noel just doled out cheerfully whatever price they asked. But the air was thick with conspiracy. An unwonted elixir of rebellion began to enliven those bleak towns. The price came down. Finally it disappeared. The wretched transportees of New Town Number One and New Town Number Two, plying the land with paint, turned in amazement to discover a throng of comrades, newly come to the barricades. People arrived with picnic lunches and with beer, with brushes and with paint. Children in pyjamas curled into sofas that were lashed in the backs of pickups, watched with staring eyes as their parents capered in the cool spring air and spread that alligator foot by foot across the sentenced land.

Then a reporter showed up, and after that a man with a fedora hat and a thick neck that seemed about to burst his tie. He wore an offended look and carried a clipboard.

*

"What did you clear on the house?" asked Gus.

"Just about nothing," said Lucy. "I had no idea we owed so much."

"Other assets?"

"A few. Rufus's estate was pretty small. I'm not going to ask Noel to sell the woods. I have enough to get through my bar admissions."

"You'll have to go to Toronto."

"A year to brush up," agreed Lucy, "and six months for bar admissions."

"The boys will stay with me."

Lucy nodded. "They might as well get used to Ottawa."

They wandered down the back lawn and climbed into the swing. It creaked loudly as it swung on its rusty pins. It was a cranky contraption. Noel had always greased it in the spring, going at it in bursts of desperation, with a lot of muttering and beseeching looks. He would set it to swing, stand back and study it, plunge in with a palmful of grease. Without this seasonal doctoring the dry bones complained through every arc.

"What surprises me is how fast our life fell apart."

"I don't think you've fallen apart," said Gus.

"Our *life*, Dad."

"Yes," he admitted.

"I knew we owed a little money. It's not that. But I'm amazed how much we rush through just to stand still."

"It's the way you live."

"No."

"Yes," he insisted. "It's the shoes you buy the boys, the way you order groceries, what you tell the dentist."

"Bill says I never buy enough food."

"You have a salmon in there, and it's fresh."

"For heaven's sake," said Lucy, "it just comes from Montreal."

"It comes from Nova Scotia," said Gus. "They fly it to Montreal."

"We had *nothing*."

Gus grinned. "This house is a wreck, but it's a very big wreck."

"Come on," said Lucy, "let's go cook the salmon. Five more minutes, and Dave will have it in the garbage."

*

The stranger was Noel. He parked his limping pickup at the road and stared at the house for several minutes. Then he shoved open the wood-and-wire gate and shambled down the path. Flecks of green paint clung to his week-old stubble. He wore a clean shirt, but his jacket and pants were stippled and striped with different shades of green. Lucy noticed him when he was halfway to the house, recognized him when he reached the door.

"I couldn't even spot your walk," she said, surprised. "You're walking differently."

"It's the boots," he said.

Lucy nodded at the heavy workboots, at Noel. "Pretty colourful, anyway. You're even making the Montreal papers."

"My alligator?"

She nodded. "I can't believe you don't want anything, Noel."

He shook his head. "Just a few things from the attic."

"There's a lot of your life in here. The more I pack, the more I find."

"Throw out what you don't want, Luce."

"Do you ever cry for me, Noel? Do you miss me?"

"I cry."

Lucy stepped closer and put her hand against her husband's rough cheek. He covered his face with his hands.

"You can't come back?" she asked.

He shook his head. Lucy clung to him, clutching his jacket in her fists and pushing her face against his chest. "We're going to let you go, darling." She touched his face again. "We're going to love you even though you've become a paint sample." They laughed. Their laughter changed to tears, returned to laughter. When they were still, Noel kissed her. He had already disappeared into the trap when the boys came in.

"Is he okay?" asked Dave when Lucy told them why the pickup was there.

"Why don't you ask him?"

"Did he hear they stopped giving me holes?" asked Bill.

"Look, guys," said Lucy. "That's your father upstairs. We love him, okay? Now go say hello."

They trooped up the back stairs and through Bill's room. Noel's ladder stood in the hall. They heard Noel scuffling but couldn't see him.

"Dad?" called Dave. There was the sound of a box being dragged across the attic beams. "Dad?" Dave called again.

Noel's head appeared in the open trap. "Hi, Dave. Hi, Bill."

"Hi," they said uncertainly.

Noel stared down at the boys. Dust clung to his whiskers. The boys eyed the rumpled, green-flecked countenance that spoke with the voice of their father.

"You don't have to be a lawyer," said Bill.

"What?" said Noel.

"Sister Mary of the Lamb of God doesn't make me get the strap any more. I own Curly, but he's pretty stupid. We're moving to Ottawa. Mom's going to be a lawyer. We'll live in Grampa's house. He's friends with the Queen. Dave and Nick are getting married."

"Shut up, Bill," said Dave.

"How are you, Dave?" asked Noel.

"I'm okay."

Noel cleared his throat. "I guess I look pretty awful."

"You look okay."

"Could you give me a hand with some of this stuff?"

Dave shot him a hurt look. "I have to help Mom," he said, and slouched away.

"He's mad at you," said Bill.

"Are you mad at me, Bill?"

Bill shook his head. "I would be delighted if you would stay to dinner."

"That's very nicely put, Bill."

"We don't have any male of the species any more, except Dave."

"You're a male yourself, Bill."

"I don't have any sperms."

"You'll get some."

"Yes," said Bill, "when I come into man's estate. I will shave and my balls will fill up with semen."

"Come on up here," said Noel.

Bill climbed up cautiously. When he got to the top Noel reached down and hauled him straight through the trap. It was dark in the attic. Noel had no flashlight. The only light came up through the trap or filtered in from outside through small circulation grates. Dry and dusty, hot, the gable attics disappeared into blackness. Bill was excited. He loved the feeling of secrecy. The attic was full of possibilities, of treasures. A few yards from where he crouched beside his father, the attic turned and vanished round a corner.

"It's nice."

"Be careful to put your weight on the two-by-fours," said Noel, "or you'll fall right through."

Noel crept round a corner. At the far end was a floored section, beneath one of the grates. A thin slash of daylight illuminated some boxes. "Is this your *stuff*?" asked Bill in wonder.

"It's just things, Bill."

He opened a box and slid out a cardboard portfolio. Untying a green ribbon, he drew out a handful of sheets and began to examine them one at a time. They were drawings. Bill sat beside him. He leaned against his father's body. Noel would squint at a drawing, then hand it to Bill. Bill received each brittle sheet with reverence, looked at it closely, set it aside. Gradually the pile beside him grew. Finally Noel finished.

"Like them?"

"They're nice," said Bill. "They don't have too many colours, though."

"Would you like them?"

"Are they yours?"

"I made them."

"I'd like them," said Bill. "I will put them on my wall."

"Would you give some to Dave?"

"Dave is pretty mad."

"Keep them," said Noel. "He might want one later."

"Time and the hour run through the roughest day," said Bill.

*

"Yves seems to be enjoying himself," said Nini listlessly. A stubby red tractor bounced across the bottom of the lawn pulling an array of mowers. The smell of cut grass blew onto the veranda. Out on Lake of Two Mountains one of the Allards' flotilla batted through the current on its way to Oka. Eleanor hunched at a desk, working her way methodically through a stack of invoices. Nini sagged in a wicker chair and followed the progress of the tractor back and forth along the water's edge.

"Possibly he would be open to some base proposal."

"Eh?" said Eleanor. "That's not Yves. Yves is a manager."

"Eh?" said Nini. The tractor roared its sturdy roar, turned, began another leg. Against the brilliant sun-enamelled water rode a silhouette of manliness. "Who is it, then?"

"A trainee."

"A lawnmower trainee?" wondered Nini.

"It's very useful," Eleanor explained. "They learn basic tractoring; we earn a tax deduction for training. Also, they are cheap."

Nini watched her sister swotting contentedly. Around them stirred the trees that had shaded them from childhood to middle age. A string of ducklings fled the approaching tractor. Nini studied Eleanor again. The thin lines around Eleanor's mouth were not unflattering, she decided. They spelt engagement, a battle. All at once Nini felt as if she were standing in the midst of a flowing dream and watching something precious draw away, not out of her life, but farther off, towards its edges.

"All of this began," she said, "for Noel."

"Lucy and the boys leave tomorrow," said Eleanor.

"It is so dreadfully sad."

"We shall have a very nice quarter," said Eleanor, shoving her glasses onto her forehead, "entirely adequate."

"I think I shall go abroad," Nini announced.

"Abroad?" Eleanor seemed to find the suggestion incomprehensible. She cast a glance of longing at her figures, before abandoning them with a sigh. "Where would you go?"

"Paris," said Nini firmly. "I believe they spend whole days leering at one another in the Bois and coughing out their lives while pale boys ravish them and weep."

For a while the sisters were silent, watching their sparkling lake, the ferry, Oka, the figure puttering back and forth on its little tractor, barbering their lawn. All down that shore white houses rode in a glitter of leaves, verandas floating on the buoyant breeze.

"You will want me to go with you," said Eleanor doubtfully.

"No."

Eleanor studied her sister. At last she put her pen aside. "I believe we had better have a look at the plum."

*

The splendid alligator, tremendous and gay, plunged across fields and into woods, writhing in serpentine majesty wherever paint would stick. It struck such gallant poses with its daggered claws and lashing blood-red tongue that the Dowager Empress of China, ascending the Dragon Throne, would not have been ashamed to have him at her side.

*

The last Swans went out of Como in the vice-regal car, with Gus and Gus's friend, behind a gold crown stamped on a crimson field. The boys were speechless at the sheer length of the car, and did not even turn as that red roof slid out of sight, Lake of Two Mountains, Charlie's mill. Into the countryside went those last Swans, upriver and away, away from gorgeous Montreal, from a Como white with dew. Nick stood at the gate and made herself not cry.

Acknowledgements

The Assyrian came down like the wolf on the fold is from "The Destruction of Sennacherib" by George Gordon, Lord Byron.

You walk in beauty, like the night is a misquote of the first lines of Byron's "She Walks in Beauty".

Earth has not anything to show more fair is from William Wordsworth's "Upon Westminster Bridge".

What light through yonder window breaks? is a partial quote of the famous line in William Shakespeare's *Romeo and Juliet.*

Thou still unravished bride of quietness, Thou foster-child of Silence and slow Time, are the opening lines of John Keats's "Ode on a Grecian Urn".

I feel a nameless sadness o'er me roll is taken from "The Buried Life", by Matthew Arnold.

Time and the hour run through the roughest day occurs in William Shakespeare's *Macbeth.*